BROWN EYES BLUE

BROWN EYES BLUE

A NOVEL

CAROLYN MEYER

BRIDGE WORKS PUBLISHING

Bridgehampton, New York

Published by Bridge Works Publishing Company, Bridgehampton, New York, an imprint of The Rowman & Littlefield Publishing Group, Inc.

Distributed in the United States by National Book Network, Lanham, Maryland. For descriptions of this and other Bridge Works books, visit the National Book Network website at www.nbnbooks.com.

FIRST PAPERBACK EDITION 2004

The characters and events in this book are fictitious. Any similarity to actual persons, living or dead, is coincidental and not intended by the author.

Library of Congress Cataloging-in-Publication Data

Meyer, Carolyn, 1935–
   Brown eyes blue : a novel / Carolyn Meyer.—1st ed.
     p. cm.
   ISBN 1-882593-68-5 (cloth : alk. paper)
   ISBN 1-882593-83-9 (pbk. : alk. paper)
1. Mothers and daughters—Fiction. 2. Middle aged women—Fiction. 3. Women painters—Fiction. 4. Pennsylvania—Fiction. 5. Nude in art—Fiction. 6. Aged women—Fiction. I. Title.

PS3563.E8724 B76 2003
813'.54—dc21

2002012674

10 9 8 7 6 5 4 3 2 1

♾ The paper used in this publication meets the minimum requirements of American National Standard for Information Sciences—Permanence of Paper for Printed Library Materials, ANSI/NISO Z39.48–1992.
Manufactured in the United States of America.

To the Class of 1953, Lewistown, Pennsylvania—
and our mothers

BROWN
EYES
BLUE

PART I

DORCAS

CHAPTER 1

It is Ruth Kauffman—"Rootie Kazootie" in the 1954 Juniata High School yearbook—who phones Dorcas with the scandal.

"Are you planning on coming home anytime soon?" Rootie asks. "For Easter, maybe?" Her Pennsylvania inflection tugs down the end of the questions. "Because I thought I'd better warn you: your mother's creating kind of a furor around here with her, uh, erotic paintings."

Dorcas, grading seventh grade book reports while watching a TV report about troops returning from the Persian Gulf, shuts her eyes. Her mother is eighty. Dorcas has expected that any day she would get a call that Lavinia had broken a hip or suffered a heart attack or a stroke, and Dorcas would rush back to do whatever was needed. But she has not anticipated anything like *this*.

"Oh," she says cautiously. "Maybe you should tell me what happened."

Rootie outlines the basic facts: the opening of the 1991 annual Art League exhibit with the elite of Juniata eager for more scenes of Amish life that have won Lavinia Buchanan an enthusiastic following since she took up painting several decades ago; instead, a dozen erotic paintings, many with nudity—frontal *male* nudity—everyone deeply shocked, Lavinia defiant, even haughty.

Dorcas can't imagine what's going on. "She seems all right otherwise?" she asks.

"Oh, yes. But maybe you ought to talk to her."

"I will," Dorcas promises. "I'll talk to her."

As soon as she gets Rootie off the phone, Dorcas calls her mother. Lavinia's voice is strong.

"I was thinking of driving out next weekend," Dorcas says. "If it's all right with you."

"Of course it's all right with me," Lavinia snaps. "Why wouldn't it be? Good excuse to have a ham. Unless you're on another of those diets."

"Ham's fine. I'll see you Thursday evening. It may be late, unless I can get someone to take my classes."

"I'll wait supper for you," her mother says. "Be careful driving."

Dorcas considers calling Gus Minor but hesitates. She's trying to break her Gus habit—Gus, who proposed three days before Christmas and then changed his mind nine days later, on New Year's Eve. "I'm not ready," he said. "I'm sorry, Dorcas. Let's just go back to the way we've been. Is that too much to ask? That we just care about each other?"

"*Yes*, it's too much to ask!" she'd cried, hurt and furious. But after a few weeks of misery, she caved in when he called her, agreed to have dinner, and then allowed things to creep back to where they'd been, which was nowhere.

Instead of Gus she phones Barbara Lambert, her former neighbor, who has been listening to her Lavinia tales for twenty-five years and her Gus Minor stories for three. "It's my mother," Dorcas says. "Apparently she's started painting male nudes. And exhibiting them. In Juniata."

Barbara lets loose a raucous laugh. "Well, good for her! So what's the big deal?"

"She's an icon in Juniata," Dorcas explains. "Icons don't go around shocking people."

"Lavinia is a gem," says Barbara. "My mother reads the obits and complains about her leaky bladder. She hasn't had a new thought since Eisenhower was president. You should be grateful."

"But this is a *scandal*, Barbara. It's not funny!"

Barbara laughs again. "You've already called Gus, I suppose."

"No. Not yet."

"Then don't. I say this as a friend."

"The friend who introduced us."

"My mistake. I'll regret it to my grave."

Ignoring sensible advice, Dorcas dials Gus. She gets a busy signal, meaning, probably, that Gus's son is on the phone. She has tried, fruitlessly, to persuade Gus to get call waiting. On the fourth or fifth try, she reaches him and repeats Ruth's story.

"Are the nudes male or female?" Gus asks, as though he's conducting an art seminar or taking a case history. "Discreet or full frontal?"

"Both. I don't know the pose, Gus." The idea that her mother might be painting penises is more than Dorcas can handle.

"You should have her meds checked," Gus advises.

"But what if it isn't her meds? What if she's going senile or something?" She wants Gus to comfort her, to reassure her, but she can tell that he's distracted. She pictures him at his desk, fiddling with his pens, arranging them by size and color.

"I wouldn't worry about it," he says. "When are you going out?"

"Next weekend." She wonders if he'll want to see her before she leaves, but he says, "Have a safe trip, Dorcas. I'll talk to you when you get back."

❧

On the corkboard above her desk hang two brown paper circles, pinned there months earlier. One day last winter, hoping to change the course of her life, Dorcas sat on her living room floor with a dinner plate from her wedding china, a brown grocery bag, a pencil, and a pair of scissors. A half-empty glass of red wine stood within reach. The exercise was the idea of her therapist, Dr. Wellborn, whom she'd started seeing when her relationship with Gus had seemed permanently stalled. One thing was already clear: Dorcas should never have picked that china. It was too formal; it didn't suit her at all.

She palmed the bag smooth on the nubby beige carpet and drew a circle, using the china plate as a pattern. She cut out the circle and, with the foot of the wineglass as a guide, drew a smaller circle inside the larger one. She cut out that one, too. Now she had a plate-sized doughnut shape with a hole in it.

According to Wellborn, this empty-circle-within-a-full-circle was supposed to represent her life. "First you fill in the big circle with all the pluses you have in your life," he instructed. "Blessings, you might call them. Then on the little circle you write the minuses, the things that are missing from your life."

"The curses," Dorcas said. "But what if there are more minuses than pluses? What if I can't squeeze all the curses on the little circle?"

"The point, Dorcas, is that everybody has a hole in his or her life, 'a hole-in-the-whole,' and your therapeutic task is to shrink the h–o–l–e and expand the w–h–o–l–e."

"How do I do that?"

"It's all a matter of perception. Please try it, Dorcas. Start with 'self' and work out from there."

"To where?"

"Oh, you know," Wellborn said vaguely. "Family, friends, lovers, job, whatever."

Last January, with her life laid out flat like a patient on a gurney, Dorcas began to work on the large circle, avoiding the ominous hole in the middle. GOOD HEALTH she printed in block letters. Her blood pressure was normal and she hadn't caught a cold in three years—not bad for fifty-four. Near that she printed NOT FAT & NOT BAD LOOKING. She crossed it out and substituted FAIRLY AT-TRACTIVE. Then she crossed out FAIRLY. No sense in being overly modest.

She reached for the wine glass, took a long swallow, and moved to another category: FAMILY.

Her daughter, Sasha, like herself, is divorced, which makes Dorcas uneasy about generational habits. Worse, Sasha lives on the opposite side of the continent in California, and Dorcas hardly ever sees her. On the other hand, with three thousand miles separating them, she and Sasha don't get on each other's nerves, the way lots of mothers and daughters do. The way Barbara's daughters drive her up the wall. The way Lavinia often does—now, for instance, with these nude paintings. *What can possibly be going on with her?*

Her father has been dead for years, but her mother is in pretty good shape for eighty—or has been until now. Dorcas has no siblings with whom to argue but also none with whom to share the responsibility of an elderly parent who lives alone, a five- to six-hour drive from Connecticut, and who is now causing a scandal. She had printed LOVEY, Sasha's name for her grandmother, and wondered if being an only child was a blessing or a curse.

Dorcas shifted her attention to the small "minus" circle. Her ex-husband lived less than ten miles away in Redding, Connecticut, with his new wife—actually not so new anymore—although Dorcas saw him only when Sasha came to visit. Alex Molnar didn't fit into her scheme of things—she hadn't used his name since they were divorced—but she decided to account for him by labeling him a "minus."

FRIENDS. Now that was a good category. In addition to Barbara, she counted several people in her folk dancing group who often invited her to parties, as well as a group of teachers in her middle school who went out for dinner together once a month and sometimes took the train to New York to see a show. Revolving in distant orbits were friends she collected throughout her life and kept in touch with at Christmas and even saw occasionally, like Ruth, who will always be Rootie, no matter what she said. In the big circle, Dorcas represented them with a cluster of stars.

WORK was more complicated. Dorcas teaches language arts to seventh and eighth graders, most of whom believe that reading sucks and writing is an obsolete and therefore useless skill. Sometimes she can't stand her students, except for the handful of bright, talented, funny kids who regularly turn up in her classes and make her feel as though it matters—as though *she* matters.

The school isn't bad, but it could be so much better if they had a decent principal instead of the insecure bitch who shoots down every innovative idea, such as Dorcas's proposal for a project that would have the kids researching and writing their family stories and would result in the publication of a nice little book. She is thinking of Aretha Jones, whose descriptions of her rambunctious family could probably end up as a novel.

"Focus on test scores," the bitch principal had said. "That's what matters. That's what parents care about." Remembering Aretha's disappointment when the project fell through, Dorcas had written Aretha's name on the big circle and the principal's name, YVONNE WILLIAMS, on the small circle of the damned.

She's still a bitch, Dorcas thinks now, and that prompts her to pour herself a glass of wine. She knows she won't get any more papers graded this afternoon anyway.

She has seven more years after this one until she can retire—seven years that feel like a prison sentence, her life ticking uselessly away, like Jacob in the Old Testament. 7 YEARS she had printed beneath Yvonne's name and drawn a cage around the words.

And when the biblical seven years were up, then what? She'd been careful with her money, her townhouse was paid off, she'd made some good investments. She had lined up a row of $$$$ on the large circle. She planned to do a lot of things: all those books she's been intending to read someday, for one thing. Getting her French up to speed, so she could read Proust in the original.

She had written BOOKS on the large circle and drawn a pair of spectacles and a quill pen.

And traveling! She's always wanted to go someplace exotic: the Seychelles, for instance, to see the lemurs. But would she really do that all by herself? Jump on a plane and head off to the Indian Ocean with just her passport and a carry-on bag? She had written it boldly—FARAWAY PLACES—and sketched a puffy cloud shape around it.

And what about HOME? Her townhouse, bought at the time of her divorce, is bland and serviceable, like the Tupperware containers Barbara once sold her, a complete set stored away in a cabinet. The townhouse was supposed to be temporary, while she sorted things out, until Sasha went away to college or until Dorcas remarried, as she assumed she would someday.

This line of thought led inevitably to Gus Minor. She had printed GUS hugely on the small circle, overlapping the other curses. GUS symbolized the great emptiness in her life, the ache of loneliness, the absence of true love. It was even possible that GUS filled the entire hole-in-the-whole, easily displacing her reluctant students and bitch principal.

Dorcas looks now at the paper circles; they're dusty and curling and nothing has improved. She's on a cruise to nowhere, and it will take a major effort to turn this boat around. So far the only positive action she's taken is to dump Wellborn.

She grips her empty wine glass so tightly that the stem snaps in two—the last of a set from her wedding gifts. Her hand is shaking when she picks up the phone again. She calls Rootie and tells her she'll be in Juniata Thursday night.

CHAPTER 2

Dorcas drives across New Jersey, peering through a windshield blurred by steady rain. The TV weather map that morning showed red and yellow patches surging across central Pennsylvania with the worst part of the storm system centered over Juniata.

She wonders what exactly she'll be getting into with this visit, besides foul weather. She hasn't lived in Juniata since she left for college in 1954. Thirty-seven years later, anxiety is still a big part of every trip home, as it has been since she was eighteen. Although Dorcas has sidled into late middle age, Lavinia finds plenty to criticize.

"I'm still your mother," Lavinia says often, "and you'll always be my little girl. Nobody else is going to tell you that skirt is too short." Or you're driving too fast, or the fabric on your new couch is enough to make a person feel woozy.

Lavinia Buchanan has lived in Juniata all her life, the last thirty-plus years as a widow. She has undergone gall bladder surgery and angioplasty, and the last time Dorcas saw her, at Thanksgiving, she'd just had a second knee replacement.

"Seems like the only time I can get you to visit is when I have something taken out or put in," Lavinia complained coyly, as if she were only kidding. Dorcas wasn't fooled.

Lavinia's eyesight and hearing seem fine, she has every one of her teeth, and she stands as straight as a rake handle. She plays bridge with "the girls," all in their seventies and eighties, on the second and fourth Thursdays and attends church every Sunday, although it's been years since she's sung in the choir. And for hours each day she paints: cornfields, farmhouses, barns, happy Amish children— and now, apparently, nude men.

Erotic nudes, Rootie said. *An oddball thing to do,* Dorcas thinks. The very words Lavinia would use.

When Dorcas was growing up, her mother worried that Dorcas was attracted to oddballs, a label Lavinia applied to people with foreign accents or hard-to-pronounce names or a fondness for things she judged exotic: poetry that didn't rhyme, food eaten with chopsticks, abstract art.

Dorcas now suspects that as much as her mother looked askance at outsiders, making acerbic comments about them in stage whispers, she was also curious to see what sort of character Dorcas might drag home next, as long as this tendency would not someday result in an unsuitable match. There was an uproar during her childhood when their Jewish doctor had the bad judgment to fall in love with his gentile nurse. When the secret marriage was revealed, Miss Polson's father cut her off without a dime and Dr. Wasserman's sisters mourned him as dead.

Dorcas was about twelve at the time, and the Wassermans' story of forbidden love thrilled her. She adored the handsome, dark-haired doctor who always took her very seriously.

"Let that be a lesson," Lavinia warned Dorcas as the Wassermans' lives went to pieces. "Stick with your own kind."

Dorcas thought of Dr. Wasserman when she brought Alex home to visit for the first time. Alex wasn't their kind either, for a long list of reasons: a foreigner with a foreign name and a foreign accent, relatives still living in a foreign country, a taste for wine and spicy sauces, manners that struck her mother as phony—all those things that attracted Dorcas and put off Lavinia. Alex certainly fit Lavinia's definition of an oddball, which may have been one of the reasons Dorcas married him.

❧

The rain has stopped, but it's dark when she reaches the outskirts of Juniata, population fifteen thousand and steady. Here on the fringes, fast food restaurants have obliterated most of her familiar landmarks. The amusement park where she went on school outings and church picnics has yielded to a Wal-Mart. Dorcas wonders what they did with the lovely old merry-go-round with the painted, prancing horses she'd ridden for countless miles.

At the top of Stafford's Hill the highway narrows and becomes Valley Street, swooping down toward Veterans Square at the center of town. Dorcas slows, watching for the monument works.

Once on the edge of town and surrounded by tidy flower beds, Juniata Marble and Granite now occupies a squat fieldstone building crowded by forlorn storefronts, houses converted to laundromats and shops selling window blinds and vacuum cleaners. The shabby sign—*Founded 1910*—needs repainting. The business began with Lavinia's father, was later taken over by Dorcas's father, Edgar Buchanan, and then run by Lavinia after Edgar's death. In her teens Dorcas spent summer vacations working in the office. She remembers when there was a real tombstone out by the curb, with SLOW DOWN—WE CAN WAIT incised in Gothic letters on its polished surface. Her father thought that was an attention getter. When Lavinia took over, she had the tombstone hauled away.

Headlights glare in her rearview mirror, and Dorcas speeds up. She should go straight to Lavinia's, but she can't resist a detour, driving past the pretty white clapboard colonial on Lindbergh Way where she grew up during World War II. There's a light on in the upstairs bedroom where she used to listen every afternoon to her favorite radio program, *Hop Harrigan, Ace of the Airwaves*. Once, a wooden swing hung from the lowest branch of the maple in the backyard; the swing is gone, the tree cut down. Dorcas always assumed that Lavinia would stay in that house, but she was wrong about that, as she was about so many of her mother's decisions.

❧

It's way past Lavinia's usual mealtime when Dorcas arrives at the apartment, but her mother has waited supper, as she promised. Lavinia's age always astonishes Dorcas; in her memory her mother appears trim, fiftyish. Lavinia's pink scalp shines through her cottony hair, thinner than Dorcas remembers but nicely cut and curled. Her body has become shapeless, as though she wears several layers of clothing. Her skin, as softly fuzzed as chamois, hangs loosely on her bones. Only the blue eyes are still youthful. Even in old age they glow like stained glass, lit from within.

Dorcas has inherited those eyes, but only the eyes are Lavinia's. The rest of Dorcas's features—the straight brown hair streaked with gray, the long face and narrow chin, the undistinguished nose—all of that comes from her father. Dorcas missed out on the wavy, honey-colored hair, the perfect teeth that she remembers from childhood, when Lavinia was in her thirties and considered a beauty.

The table by the bay window is set with linen placemats and the good china and silver usually reserved for guests. Dorcas still feels like a guest in this apartment, where her mother has lived for a decade. You'd think she'd be used to it by now, but Dorcas has never gotten over being home-sick for Lindbergh Way, the maple tree, her small, white, comforting bed.

The food is familiar, predictable: tuna noodle casserole and iceberg lettuce with orange-colored dressing. Lavinia has never been much of a cook, and this is her standby meal. Dorcas wonders if it's possible to buy any kind of let-tuce in Juniata but iceberg. She pictures herself walking into Giant Super and asking for mesclun, imagines the blank look on the produce manager's face. But she is fam-ished and eats ravenously.

"Have you heard from Sasha?" Lavinia inquires.

"I talked to her on her birthday a few weeks ago. She sounded fine."

"I sent her a birthday card and a *very* nice check," Lavinia says, thin-lipped. "I haven't heard a single word from her." She slaps the table for emphasis.

Dorcas understands that her mother is blaming her for not teaching Sasha good manners, but she doesn't rise to the bait. "She's so busy, you know, but I'm sure she'll write," Dorcas says, although she's sure she won't unless she's reminded. Dorcas begins to stack their dishes. "Shall I make coffee?"

While the decaf drips, she washes the two Spode plates and monogrammed forks, and Lavinia dries them and puts the plates in the china closet and the forks in the felt-lined silver chest, little chores that keep them occupied.

"What do you hear from Alex?" Lavinia asks.

"Nothing. I never hear from Alex."

Lavinia arranges Pepperidge Farm cookies on a cut-glass plate. "They sent me that for Easter," she says, indicating a pot of red tulips on a table by the sofa. "Alex and his new wife, what's-her-name. Ellen."

They have been divorced for thirteen years, Alex has been married to his "new wife" for nine, yet Lavinia still asks about him as though he were part of Dorcas's daily life. Dorcas pours two cups of coffee. "Thoughtful of them," she says, although she's unreasonably irritated by those tulips.

"Well, Dorcas," Lavinia says, when they're back at the table, "tell me your news. You look all right—too thin, a person with a long face like yours shouldn't let herself get too thin, it's aging, but otherwise you look pretty good. What about that man who asked you to marry him and then got cold feet? Has he changed his mind again?"

Dorcas struggles to keep her expression and her voice neutral. "No," she says. "And there's no chance he will. But I wouldn't marry him now even if he did."

"No?" Lavinia cocks her head. "Too bad. Must be hard for you. It's not easy for a person your age to find a man."

A little electric jolt of anger surges through Dorcas. "Well," she says, "you never married again after Daddy died, and your life has been just fine, so why should I?"

"Because you're different," Lavinia says matter-of-factly, as though that should be obvious. Her bright lipstick has leaked into the tiny creases around her mouth. "You need a man."

"Oh? And what makes you think that?"

"Now don't be so touchy." Lavinia selects a cookie and bites off a corner. "There's nothing wrong with that. I'm not saying there is. It's just that you make different decisions than I would." She balances the rest of the cookie perfectly on the saucer so that it won't slide when she lifts her cup. Lavinia is an expert at such moves.

They are careening toward an argument. "Anything new at church?" Dorcas asks, shifting toward safer territory. It's much too soon to bring up her mother's paintings, the waters too choppy for such a fragile craft to be launched. "How's the new minister working out?"

"Ha!" Lavinia exclaims. "Wait till you hear this one!" And she's off on a tirade about Reverend Burkholder, who refused to move his family into the parsonage adjoining the church building but rented a house elsewhere and then had the nerve to ask the church to pay for it. "'We need privacy,' that's what he said! Can you beat that?" Lavinia cries. "I'm thinking of cutting back my pledge, if they let him get away with it."

Dorcas listens patiently. "Maybe he'll change his mind."

"That'll be the day."

Dorcas tries a different tack. "Have you sold any paintings lately?" she asks, a harmless question although paddling dangerously close to the falls.

"I could sell most of what I paint, if I wanted to," Lavinia says, chin lifted. "Had a show a couple of weeks ago. Did I tell you about that?"

Dorcas is delighted—her mother has introduced the subject herself! "You mentioned something about it. How did it go?"

"Very well," says Lavinia smugly. "It was very well attended."

And that's it. She stops there.

Knowing that she may not find a better opening and anxious to get it over with, Dorcas forges ahead. "Mother," she begins, "I have a confession to make. I came to see *you*, of course, but I also came because I heard about your new paintings. Some people are apparently concerned—"

"Busybodies," Lavinia growls. She snatches up another cookie and reduces it to crumbs. "*Some* people say they're lewd, which is certainly not true. There's nothing lewd about those paintings, because there's nothing lewd about the human body. I would have thought that *you*, Dorcas, *of all people*—"

She stops abruptly. Furiously she sweeps the crumbs into the palm of her hand and flings them into the sink.

Dorcas lets the "you of all people" part slide past and tries again.

"Mother, you can paint whatever you like. But maybe you need to think about whether you really want to put some of the more, uh, controversial paintings on exhibit, that's all."

No response. Lavinia sniffs and looks away. Dorcas studies her mother's knobby fingers.

"Where are the paintings?" Dorcas ventures.

"In a safe place."

"Will you show them to me?"

"You'll see them at the proper time."

The rain, which has started again, slaps the dark windows. Neither speaks. The clock on the courthouse steeple strikes nine. Lavinia sighs.

"Dorcas, I hope you don't mind if I leave you alone, but I can't keep my eyes open another minute. I'm going to say good night and see you in the morning. The sofa bed's all made up."

"No, I don't mind," Dorcas says, maybe a little too quickly. "I think I'll run over and say hello to Ruth Kauffman. Rootie."

"It's raining hard."

"I've got an umbrella."

"You won't stay out late?" It's phrased as a question, but Dorcas knows better.

"No, no. I'll be back by eleven. I'm pretty tired, too."

"You have a key?"

"Yes."

"Be sure to lock the door, will you? You have to turn the key to the right *twice*, remember."

"I remember."

"Say hello to Rootie for me."

CHAPTER 3

Rootie's husband, Billy, was killed in a car crash in the 1970s, a sensation because another woman was with him and everyone knew they'd been having an affair. Rootie had to sell their beautiful old place in the country to pay off Billy's gambling debts, which she didn't know about either. Since then she's lived in a narrow half of a double house down the street from the county library, where she works.

The rain has tapered off and Dorcas walks the six blocks to Rootie's, stopping by the state store to pick up a bottle of sherry. Rootie hugs her and looks her up and down.

"You never change a bit," she says.

Rootie herself is still pretty much the same as she was in high school—Rootie Kazootie with the naturally curly hair and the infectious laugh—plus a now too-obvious dye job, bifocals in frames that look as though she's got them upside down, and thirty extra pounds.

Rootie's house is clammy; the thermostat must be set at sixty. She wears a lumpy sweater buttoned to the neck and sheepskin slippers shaped like a pair of small rabbits. She produces two juice glasses and pours a cautious inch of sherry into each. She settles onto a red vinyl La-Z-Boy. Dorcas curls up on the worn sofa. A gray cat strolls in and Dorcas glares at it, willing it not to come any closer. They raise their glasses: "Cheers." Dorcas counts on the sherry to warm her up.

Rootie pops up the footrest on her recliner. "So how's that guy, Gus? I thought for sure you'd be married by now."

"For a few days, so did I," Dorcas says with a shaky laugh.

"Didn't you go off to Florida or someplace with him at Christmas, while I was sitting here worrying about whether we'd end up in a war with Iraq? Mikey's in the reserves, you know."

Dorcas is stricken; she'd forgotten about Rootie's son. "Was he called up?"

Rootie shakes her head. "So tell me."

"Here's how it went: three days before Christmas, he asked me to marry him. It was all very romantic. Of course I said yes—I'd only been waiting for this for three years. We flew to Florida on the twenty-eighth, and on New Year's Eve he told me he couldn't go through with it. He wanted to go back to where we had been. Square One."

"Please don't tell me you agreed."

"Not at first. But—you know how it is."

Rootie nods. "You've known him for how long?"

"Four years. Three and a half, actually."

"God, Dorcas. How come you don't just dump him?"

"I've tried. Then he calls and I give in. He's charming, he's attractive, he's intelligent, he's a shit."

"And you are weak."

"I hate being alone."

"Don't we all." Rootie sips her sherry. "How's Sasha?"

"Fine, as far as I know. Lavinia's pissed because Sasha didn't send her a thank-you note for her birthday check, and I think I'm supposed to feel guilty about that."

Rootie laughs. "Speaking of Lavinia!"

"Yes, please tell me!" Dorcas says. "What has my mother been up to? I couldn't get anything out of her."

Rootie holds out her glass and Dorcas pours her a generous slug. "Well, you know how everybody loves Lavinia," Rootie begins, and Dorcas nods—she's been hearing it for years. "And around here, at least, she's made quite a name for herself with her paintings. Everybody looks forward to the Juniata Art League's annual show, because Lavinia's just about the biggest talent we've got since Morris Cleveland died. Of AIDS, but nobody's supposed to know that." Rootie pauses to light a cigarette. "I know, I know. I promised Mikey and Denise I'd quit. But a person's surely entitled to one vice, isn't she?"

"Lavinia would agree with that. She still smokes—I can smell it in her apartment." In high school Rootie was always snitching her brother's Luckys; every time Dorcas tried smoking, she felt like throwing up. It took Dorcas years to learn, even longer to stop.

"This year your mother announced that she'd been working on a new series, and she made the League people promise that she could hang them herself and keep them covered until the opening, when she'd personally unveil them. A surprise. The show was in the lobby of the old Coleman Hotel. You know it isn't a hotel anymore? That it's been converted to senior apartments?"

"I heard. Too bad, isn't it?" Dorcas remembers Sunday dinners at the Coleman. She always ordered chicken and waffles, and her parents had the roast beef, well done.

"Yeah, but it looks pretty nice. I wouldn't mind living there myself. Anyway, Lavinia insisted on absolute secrecy and they humored her, because she's who she is and the founder of the League and so on. So Lavinia gets this boy,

Charlie Benner—Rod Benner's nephew. You remember Rodney, a year ahead of us? Married Marlene Ulsh? Only they're split now. Charlie does yard work and chores for Lavinia. Well, he has his license, so he hauls her and her paintings over to the Coleman real early in the morning, before anybody's around, and the two of them hang the paintings and cover them up with sheets."

"When *was* this?" Dorcas asks, wondering why Lavinia didn't invite her if it was such a big deal.

"Exactly four weeks tomorrow they had the opening, with wine and cheese and vegetables with ranch dip. The artsy crowd all turned out—you'd probably know a lot of them. There was your mother, looking elegant as all get-out in a lavender suit and a string of pearls that I'd bet are the real thing, her hair just done—Marlene Benner still does it for her. Lots of people go to her, me included. With that silver-headed cane Lavinia's started carrying, she's definitely the Queen Bee, you know? So when she's got everyone's attention, she starts peeling the sheets off the paintings, one by one. A real flair for drama.

"The first half dozen are Amish farms, her usual style, and she gets a big round of applause. Then comes one with a barn and a couple of cows and horses and two people standing under a tree, a man and a woman—but they're not wearing Amish clothes, they're *naked*, like Adam and Eve."

"Oh, now really, Rootie, who could object—?"

"Well, listen. We're just getting started here. Everybody kind of chuckles, you know—indulgently. But the next one is a painting of two nudes, both women, one young and the other older. And the younger one is posing for the older one, who's standing at an easel, painting. Nothing left to the imagination in that one, if you get what I mean."

"Lesbians?" Dorcas feels a little lightheaded. No wonder everyone in Juniata is up in arms.

"Well, I don't think so, although a lot of other people do. More like it was the same woman, only at different stages. Now it's a really good painting, although I'm probably not any judge, but by then people are getting pretty uncomfortable, and there's just a polite smattering of applause. Then she gets to the next-to-last one. Off comes the sheet, and it's a guy, stark naked. Not a stitch on! And I don't mean a discreet pose, you know, with the thigh kind of hiding everything, or even a back view of his buns." Rootie swings her legs off the La-Z-Boy and stands up to demonstrate. "Full frontal, Dorcas! You could see his thing, his curly black pubic hair, everything! And he's standing there, looking out of the painting straight at you, and his right hand is reaching out and he's smiling, as though he's inviting you to . . ."

Rootie sinks heavily onto the recliner. The gray cat rockets onto her lap. Dorcas's tongue sits uselessly in her mouth.

"We all just gasped. And *then*, Dorcas, while everybody is standing there, too surprised to know what to say, Lavinia whips off the last drape. Here's this couple, I'm sure it's the same guy, dark-haired and handsome, and a girl, I think the same girl in the portrait, blond, and they're—doing it."

"Doing it?" Dorcas echoes dumbly. "You mean—fucking?"

"Uh-huh."

Stunned, Dorcas gasps. "I can't believe this," she says. "So what happened next? After she unveiled the last picture?"

"Well, at that point Dr. Wilson, the chief of staff out at the hospital? And Sam Larber, the lawyer? He and his wife rush around putting the sheets back up again, over the three nude paintings. I think they left Adam and Eve uncovered. Then Harriet Stamm, who organized the show, and her husband, Don, take your mother aside and tell her this isn't at all appropriate. I was standing right there, I heard every word. And Lavinia, bless her heart, looking very dignified, says, 'It's art, and therefore it is appropriate.' Everybody starts arguing, and the Stamms decide to close the exhibit until they can make a decision about how to handle the thing legally. But the *Sentinel* had sent a reporter and a photographer to cover the event, and did they ever go bananas!

"Next, the letters to the editor start pouring in. Some people thought she'd gotten Charlie Benner to pose for her, and they wanted to investigate possible sexual abuse of a minor. The Council of Churches wanted her to resign from the board of the Art League—the league she founded! Then a couple of weeks ago the *Harrisburg Times-Patriot* did a feature on her—I saved a copy for you—and I heard the *Philadelphia Inquirer* was sending a reporter and a photographer up to investigate. If it keeps on this way, Lavinia could end up on *Larry King*. She didn't tell you any of this?"

Dorcas fishes a Kleenex out of her pocket and blows her nose. "I knew about the exhibit, that she'd been painting a lot to get ready for it. I didn't know about the 'new work' until you called me. I did get something out of her a little while ago. She admits that some people think the paintings are lewd, but that's all she'd say."

Dorcas has been worrying with her fingernail at a split in the upholstery of Rootie's aged couch and has managed to make the split bigger. "But think about this, Rootie: Would anybody have made this kind of fuss if the artist was someone Sasha's age, say? Or an eighty-year-old *man*? Picasso, for instance. They're probably making her out to be a dirty old woman, right? A pervert?"

"Right."

"But are the paintings really—dirty? You know, obscene?"

"You'll have to decide that yourself. I admit I was shocked, but that's because it was so unexpected. I mean who'd have thought that Lavinia—?"

"Not me, that's for damn sure. Do you remember how we used to put a glass up to the bedroom wall to try to hear if our parents were doing it in the next room? And I never heard anything, because my parents slept in separate rooms. My mother frowned on sex, for God's sake!"

Rootie snickers. The sherry glass rests on her stomach. "I also remember how you used to keep track of Edgar's rubbers."

Dorcas feels her face get hot. Every week when she put away her father's laundry, she'd sneak out the box of Trojans he kept hidden under his balled-up black socks and count them. None was ever missing.

She gets up and walks around Rootie's cramped living room, struggling with this new view of her mother. "There's something that worries me—do you really think the guy in the painting is Charlie? Because that *could* be serious."

Rootie has lowered the La-Z-Boy to a semi-reclining position, and she gazes up at Dorcas from this oblique angle. "No, for a couple reasons. First, the face definitely isn't Charlie's—Charlie has light brown hair and blue eyes, and the guy in the painting has dark hair and brown eyes. He's older, and the build is different, too. Except for the eyes, it looks a little like Morris Cleveland. You remember *him*, don't you?"

"I never met him, but I've been hearing about Morris for years, ever since Mother started taking art lessons from him."

"Funny you never met. He and Lavinia were very close. But I don't think it's Morris, because I got a chance to look at the labels she put up next to the paintings. The picture of the male was titled 'Nicholas,' and she called the couple 'Nicholas in Love.' Who's Nicholas?"

"Nicholas?" Dorcas scratches around in her memory for that name and draws a blank.

⁂

It's close to midnight when Dorcas slips quietly into her mother's studio. The room was once a sleeping porch, converted when Lavinia bought the house and had it made over into a duplex, the upstairs into an apartment for herself, the downstairs into offices currently rented to an optometrist. One door to the studio is from Lavinia's bedroom, but there's a second door, reached through the bathroom.

Edgar's old rolltop desk takes up one end of the long, narrow studio. Dorcas pads softly to the opposite end, where Lavinia keeps her easel. Propped on it is a painting of a one-room schoolhouse with Amish children playing ball in the schoolyard while the teacher stands in the doorway, ringing a bell.

She stoops down to look through canvases stacked along the wall—a horse and gray-topped buggy trotting down a country lane, men in broad-brimmed black hats at a barn raising, a circle of women in dark dresses and white caps bent over a quilting frame. No sign of any nudes.

Then Dorcas thinks of the cedar closet in the hall next to Lavinia's bedroom. Listening to the steady rhythm of her mother's snore with the little whistle at the top, she opens the closet door and pulls the chain of an overhead light. Several coats and jackets hang on a rod. Dorcas is about to close the door when it occurs to her that the closet used to be much deeper. She gropes behind the clothes and discovers a pair of closely fitted panels, fastened with a lock. On a hunch she goes back to the studio, slides up the top of Edgar's desk, and finds the secret drawer that she remembers from childhood. In it is a small brass key.

Her hands are sweating, and she feels nervous and guilty and excited, just as she did when she was a teenage snoop, counting condoms. What if her mother gets up to go to the bathroom and finds her here? Nevertheless, she unlocks the panel and slides it open.

The closet has been fitted to hold paints, brushes, blank canvases; at the back of the closet more than a dozen paintings are stored in a row of narrow slots. One by one Dorcas pulls them out and holds them to the light. *Here they are.*

They're exquisite, the nude figures strongly modeled but tender. She comes to the double portrait that Rootie described. It's actually triple—one nude woman painting another, and a third woman emerging on the artist's canvas, a painting within a painting.

Dorcas can easily identify the women. She has on a shelf at home a collection of family photographs, including her parents' wedding picture, and, faded to sepia, a studio portrait of Lavinia in her teens that makes the most of her finely chiseled features, light-colored curls falling to her shoulders, eyes pale and mysterious as icebergs. In the painting the artist is an aging Lavinia, hair fading and breasts sagging. The model is the very young Lavinia, and the woman emerging on the artist's canvas is Lavinia the bride. All three Lavinias are strong, sensual women.

The nude male in the second painting is startling, beautiful and enigmatic: dark-haired, brown-eyed, olive-skinned, his thick cock uncircumcised. The man is definitely not Edgar Buchanan. Dorcas has no idea who this Nicholas was. She is sure that Lavinia will not tell her, even if she dares to ask.

The third painting, of Nicholas and a girl who is certainly the young Lavinia, is riveting. The two are entwined, in ecstasy, but there's an aspect that Rootie didn't mention: the woman is a half-finished statue, and her lover is the sculptor, still creating his masterpiece even as he makes love to her.

On the other side of the wall, Lavinia murmurs and seems to chuckle in her sleep. Dorcas flicks out the light and waits, breathing shallowly. Then she slips out of the hidden closet and locks it, arranges the coats and jackets to conceal the panel, and returns the brass key to the secret drawer. She changes into pajamas and hauls open the sofa bed, sheets and blanket tidily in place. She lies there, sleepless, thinking of the paintings.

It's Nicholas who keeps Dorcas awake: Who *was* he? What became of him?

CHAPTER 4

Morning arrives in a sluggish aftermath of too much sherry, too much thinking; Dorcas wakes too early, her throat aching from a throttled dream. Fumbling for the light, she nearly knocks over Alex's tulips. When did he start sending Lavinia flowers? More likely it wasn't Alex at all, but Ellen.

Still in pajamas, she watches Lavinia eat a bowl of raisin bran with hot water instead of milk. "Isn't there something you can take for lactose intolerance?" Dorcas asks. "Lactaid or something?"

"Thank you, but I *prefer* it this way. I've never liked milk. I bought you a quart, though. Help yourself." Lavinia eyes Dorcas piercingly. "You look terrible," she declares. "Bags under your eyes halfway down to your knees. What time did you get back from Rootie's?"

"Not late." Dorcas stretches elaborately and looks out the window into Lavinia's backyard, brown, leafless, and soggy. At least it's not raining. "If it's all right with you, I think I'll go for a walk. See what's new in town."

"I can tell you the answer to *that* one: Nothing. But go on. I haven't finished yesterday's crossword puzzle."

"No painting today?" Dorcas asks, hoping the question sounds casual.

That sharp look again. "I always paint in the afternoon. The light's better."

Dorcas pulls on sweats and a nylon shell and starts down the stairs. "Are you going to be warm enough in that?" Lavinia calls out. Dorcas remembers the scratchy sweaters she had to wear as a child, the rubber overshoes that made her feet sweat. And scarves, always scarves, around her neck, over her head, across her nose and mouth.

"I'm fine, Mother. I'll see you in about an hour."

"Dorcas!" Lavinia hollers. "What about gloves?"

⚜

Elbows pumping, Dorcas strides up Market Street past what is left of Juniata's nineteenth-century brick buildings, crowded and stained like bad teeth. The old mansard roofs slope down to meet the 1960s facades of shoe shops and clothing stores. Across the street is the Trolley Stop, formerly Jack's Bar & Grill. When Dorcas was a kid, she hurried past it, alarmed by the ominous rumble of men's voices but glancing in furtively to glimpse dark shapes hunched on bar stools. In its new incarnation as a diner, there are ruffled curtains at the windows and plastic flowers on each table. It's one of Lavinia's favorites. She's fond of their daily specials and of Wanda, the waitress who entertains her with hard-luck stories.

Wasserman's Ladies Shop, once owned by the doctor's two spinster sisters, is long gone, although the ghosts of the brass letters are still visible on the marble fascia. A faded

For Rent sign is taped to the window, a pile of trash sags against the door.

In the next block Dorcas stops for a look into People's Drugs, where her father drank his morning coffee every day except Sunday. He'd order one cup, black, exchange a few words with other regulars, and then he was on his way to Juniata Marble and Granite. The green-veined counter and soda fountain have been replaced by a rack of greeting cards. He always let Dorcas come with him when she had no school. Dorcas misses him as sharply as if he'd just left.

One of her biggest regrets is that her father didn't live to see Sasha. At the time of Edgar's death, Dorcas and Alex had been married for three years and she still hadn't gotten pregnant. All those years of being terrified of getting knocked up (Lavinia: *The worst thing a girl can do to her parents*) and then, when she was safely a wife and wanted a baby more than she'd ever wanted anything, nothing happened. It would be another five years until her miracle baby was born. They named her Alexandra Lavinia but called her Sasha from the day they brought her home from the hospital.

Lavinia was fifty-two when Edgar died in 1962. Dorcas remembers her mother's exhaustion from nursing him through those last awful months, her grief ("Thank God he never had to deal with dirty hippies") when finally he was gone. Then came a sudden change. A few weeks after the funeral she took over Edgar's rolltop desk—it had originally been her father's and smelled of brandy and cigars—and announced that from then on *she* would run Juniata Marble and Granite. "My father started this business," Lavinia informed Dorcas. "It was understood that it would be mine someday."

Was it? Dorcas doesn't remember that; she assumed—incorrectly—that Lavinia would simply sell it.

After Lavinia got rid of the SLOW DOWN—WE CAN WAIT tombstone, she had the offices repainted, replaced the run-down furniture with reproductions of antiques, and kept the rolltop desk. The business flourished. Dorcas doubts that her mother ever stopped at People's for coffee on her way to the office; Lavinia always disliked sitting at a counter. She realizes what a young, energetic widow her mother must have been, younger than Dorcas is now. She envies her, in a way.

When Lavinia turned seventy, she sold the monument business to one of Edgar's nephews. Next she sold the house on Lindbergh Way, never saying a word to Dorcas until she'd already made up her mind. Dorcas always thought she'd inherit that house, although she had no idea what she'd do with it.

Lavinia bought the squarish tan brick house a block south of Veterans Square and hired Rodney Benner, Dorcas's high school friend, to remodel it. Dorcas argued against her moving into the upstairs—Lavinia was having trouble with her knees—and tried to persuade her that she could live much more conveniently on the first floor.

Lavinia brushed aside these objections. "The downstairs is just too dark," she said. "But if it makes you feel better, I'll have Rodney put in a lift." Now Lavinia rides up the long stairway on a little electrically operated seat.

Dorcas passes the Emporium, where Lavinia bought her her first bra and the music store where she used to buy sheet music, songs she heard on the radio sung by Jo Stafford, Nat King Cole. At Five Points she turns toward the river onto Chestnut Street, a pretty street of big trees and old houses that began a gentle decline a quarter century ago, long after Dorcas left Juniata.

In the middle of the third block she halts in front of the stately red brick house where her high school boyfriend, Jimmy O'Brien, used to live. Jimmy, who became a Catholic priest, died in his thirties; Lavinia clipped the obituary from the *Sentinel*, wrote "kidney failure" across the top, and mailed it to Dorcas.

The house stands empty now, a weathered *For Sale* sign tilted against the rusting iron fence. Tangled shrubbery clots the triangular wedge of yard overlooked by twin bay windows on the west side. Shutters hang loose or are missing. Blistered green paint, streaked with bird shit, is peeling from the handsome double doors. The brass hardware is gone, leaving deep gouges where screws used to be. The marble steps have sunk at an angle, and the wrought-iron railing gives under Dorcas's hand as she leans over it, trying to peer through a cracked window.

In the dusky light she can make out the fireplace. Its delicately curved mantel was once crowded with photographs of Jimmy's father, a navy surgeon lost when his ship went down in the South Pacific. Jimmy's older sister, Maryanne, married before she finished high school and had a slew of kids by a husband who wasn't thought to be worth much. They all lived with Jimmy and his widowed mother.

The graceful staircase with its carved banister rises from the center hall. When Dorcas was seventeen, Jimmy once managed to smuggle her up those creaking stairs to his room in the back. They necked feverishly for a few minutes until noisy footsteps and muffled giggling broke out at the keyhole of Jimmy's door. The two remained trapped, petrified, until Maryanne hollered for the kids to come to supper, and they whooped and clattered down the uncarpeted stairs.

"Stay here, Dorcas," Jimmy had whispered urgently. "I'm going down. Wait until we've been at the table long enough to say grace, then you sneak out."

He left her standing alone in the dark until she got up the nerve to bolt for the front door. They broke up soon after graduation, when Jimmy left for the seminary. Dorcas has not been in that house since.

Going on forty years, she figures.

Dorcas memorizes the phone number on the *For Sale* sign and heads back to Lavinia's. Just out of curiosity, she'd like to see the inside of the house again. Just out of curiosity, she'd like to know how much they're asking for it.

༺✦༻

"Good Lord!" Lavinia exclaims when Dorcas mentions that she's made an appointment to look at the O'Briens' old house. "What for?"

"For fun," Dorcas says, although that's not quite the truth. She isn't sure exactly why she wants to go through the old house. "Why don't you come with me?"

"No *thank you*," Lavinia says firmly, and after lunch, while Lavinia "rests her eyes," Dorcas goes alone.

"You know its history?" inquires the saleswoman in the green wool suit and fake nails. She doesn't seem to mind taking a client to look at a forsaken house on the afternoon of Good Friday when virtually every business in Juniata is closed. Her name is Sharon Dieter, and she grins when Dorcas introduces herself. "Your mother is the artist, right? I'm a big fan of her paintings." Dorcas wonders if she saw the exhibit or knows about the embarrassing scandal, but she says nothing.

Sharon consults her notes. "The house was built in 1870 by William Alfred Morgan, who owned an iron foundry here in Juniata. He was the wealthiest man in town, and this was at that time one of our finest residences."

The house smells of dampness and must. Its previous owners, coming after the O'Briens, divided the high-ceilinged rooms into awkward, dingy apartments, squirrels gnawed through the walls and romped in Jimmy's old bedroom, and somebody lit a fire in the parlor fireplace without opening the damper. Pigeons have squeezed through a broken pane of one of the tall, graceful windows in the dining room and perched on the mantel. Their white droppings dapple the marble hearth.

Sharon pats her stiff, coppery hair and points out the fine cherry wood banister. "Now you can see that it does need a lot of work," Sharon says. "But what potential, especially for someone with imagination. Someone like yourself. And we haven't looked at the old stable, out back. They're only asking eighty-nine five, and I think there's some room there to negotiate. It's been on the market for quite some time."

Dorcas runs her fingers over the smooth cherry wood, feeling the fine detail of its carving. The house is as cold as an underground cavern, but the warmth of the wood spreads through her hands and up her arms. Later, when she tries to explain to her friends—to Rootie, to Barbara, even to Gus—why she made her completely irrational decision, she talks about that moment when her hand was on the cherry wood banister: "I felt connected, somehow," she tells them. "It just felt right."

Dorcas spends a longer time at the old house than she intended, but certainly—she realizes this later—not long enough. Too much time savoring details of window moldings and cornices, not enough time on the wheezing furnace and collapsing gutters. Through the decay and ruin an image has begun to emerge of Morgan House restored to splendor. She walks through the rooms, mentally replacing layers of peeling wallpaper with shades of Wedgwood and rose and ripping up the matted shag carpet to reveal the burnished maple floors that Sharon claims lie beneath. Swept up in a fantasy, she forgets about her faithless lover, her bitch principal; she even forgets about her mother's paintings and the mysterious Nicholas.

"I've always thought," Sharon says, trailing after her, "that this place would make a terrific bed-and-breakfast. I've even checked out the zoning, and there's no problem."

Yes! Dorcas can see it, too! Rested from a night's sleep in the elegant upstairs bedrooms, contented guests sit in the gracious dining room, spreading clotted cream and raspberry jam on scones hot from the oven. There are roses from the garden on the mantel, Mozart in the background. Conversation sparkles. And there she is, Dorcas herself, smilingly pouring coffee.

With an effort Dorcas banishes the fantasy. "This is ridiculous," she mutters, half aloud. To Sharon she says, "Let's go."

Sharon smiles brightly. "I have a number of interesting listings. Places that don't need as much work as this one. Are you planning on moving back here soon?"

"I'm not planning anything," Dorcas confesses. *Except dealing with my mother and her erotic paintings.*

CHAPTER 5

Lavinia perches on a stool in her studio, working on a painting of a young Amish couple in an open buggy. A sliver of moon hangs over a barn, and a man in a broad-brimmed black hat stands silhouetted in the golden light of the barn door.

"Sweet, isn't it?" Lavinia asks, leaning back for a better angle. "On their way home from a singing."

"Charming," Dorcas agrees, but her attention is drawn to the faces: the dark-haired boy wearing a straw hat, the blond, blue-eyed girl in a bonnet. "Don't mind me," Dorcas says. "May I look at some of your other paintings?"

"Help yourself," her mother murmurs and dabs at the spokes of the buggy wheels.

Dorcas flips again through the canvases stacked along the walls and sees plainly now what she didn't notice the night before. There is nothing erotic about these Amish folks, the farmers and their wives and children in traditional garb, going about their traditional lives. But in every one of them she can see the faces of Nicholas and Lavinia. She sees their eyes.

❧

"So," says Lavinia as they're fixing dinner—chicken thighs and a shared baked potato—"tell me about the O'Brien place. It's a shambles, isn't it?"

"A total ruin." But she doesn't say that she can now think of nothing else, of how beautiful it could be. She realizes, with dismay, that she's falling in love—with a house this time, not a man. It's the kind of thing that could swallow up the brown paper circle pinned above her desk, overwhelm the hole-in-the-whole. She knows that her mother has guessed she's up to something, and she almost confesses. But she can't. Not yet.

After they've eaten, Dorcas drives Lavinia to church for the Good Friday service. This is the church where Edgar and Lavinia were married, where they took Dorcas to be baptized as an infant at the white marble font donated by her grandfather. The oak railing where Dorcas knelt on the day of her confirmation, self-conscious about the nylon stockings and garter belt she was wearing for the first time. She walked down this aisle on her wedding day, clutching her father's arm, toward the altar where the minister and Alex and his best man, his cousin Toby, waited for her. Three years later Edgar's coffin was placed in front of that altar, surrounded by dozens of floral arrangements; Dorcas has hated gladioli ever since. Eventually it was Sasha's turn to be baptized here.

The minister—she supposes he is the one who needs privacy for his family—fondles his wispy beard as he preaches to a sparse congregation on sin and forgiveness. Dorcas wonders if he was one of the members of the Council of Churches who, offended by Lavinia's paintings, called for her resignation from the League.

Dorcas's mind wanders during the sermon, wanders all the way back to Jimmy O'Brien. The crush she had on him must have driven Lavinia to despair. Lavinia probably wasn't much concerned about sex at that stage; it was the lure of the Catholic Church that made her nervous. Lavinia was right to be afraid: Dorcas got Jimmy to teach her how to pray the rosary, and when she was sixteen she set up a secret altar in the back of her closet with a couple of votive candles and a little statue of the Virgin Mary. She intended to convert, as soon as she could persuade her parents to allow it or was old enough to do it without their permission. She would marry Jimmy but she would not use birth control. The romance with both Jimmy and the church fizzled out, but she still remembers how to pray the rosary: *Hail Mary, full of grace, the Lord is with thee . . .*

The sermon ends and the congregation stands to recite prayers. Dorcas and Lavinia share a hymnal and sing: *O Sacred Head, now wounded, With grief and shame weighed down.* Dorcas did this for all the years of her growing up, until she left for college. Lavinia's voice quavers and cracks on the sustained notes.

"Thank you," Lavinia says on the way home. "I don't go out at night anymore unless somebody takes me."

Dorcas watches her mother walk unsteadily into her bedroom. In the doorway Lavinia turns and blows a kiss. She looks weary, even frail. "Are you going to Rootie's?"

"I thought I might."

"Don't stay out too late. You look a little peaked."

❧

"You're crazy, Dorcas," says Rootie. "Out of your frigging mind." They are again in Rootie's living room, same places, same glasses, more sherry. "You're not actually serious about buying that house, are you?"

"I just said I'm *thinking* about it."

"Have you told Lavinia yet?"

"No."

"What on earth made you decide to do this?"

"I told you: I haven't decided anything."

But in fact she has, and she is still trying to figure out why she had made up her mind in less than eight hours that she wants to buy the ruined old house and move back to Juniata. Restore it and open a bed-and-breakfast. She's even got a name for it: Morgan House.

Rootie's right: she's crazy.

She tries to explain the feeling she had when she put her hand on the banister, how she felt that she belonged in that house. "I stood in that awful, filthy kitchen," she says, "and I swear I could smell bread baking, and apple pies. And upstairs, it was the oddest thing, in those ugly old bed-rooms, I thought I could smell lemons."

"*Lemons?*" Rootie isn't buying any of it. "Sounds like a hallucination to me. You haven't been hearing voices, have you?"

"It feels like the right thing to do," Dorcas says, hands lifted helplessly. "I need a change."

"A bed-and-breakfast in Juniata! Now I've heard every-thing." Rootie shakes her head. "So now what do you do?"

"Make a ridiculously low offer and see what happens."

"Hand it over to Fate, in other words."

"Exactly." Dorcas holds the sherry bottle up to the light and divides the last few ounces between the two glasses. "It's like falling in love with someone you know will be nothing but trouble. Like Gus Minor, who has obviously been hopeless from the day I met him. It just took me too long to admit it." She rubs her forehead, trying to erase thoughts of Gus. "But, Rootie, a house can be remodeled, rejuvenated, brought back from the brink of ruin. A man can't! And God knows I've tried—probably harder than I should have with Gus, maybe not as hard as I should have with Alex."

"You're buying this ruin because you don't know how to get rid of a guy?"

"Because I want to change my life. And because maybe Lavinia needs a change, too. Maybe she needs me."

Rootie's penciled eyebrows creep upward. "So, do you think she's gotten a little—unbalanced? That the paintings are a sign?"

"Actually, she seems completely normal. But she's *old*. It might be a good idea if I were around. Handy." Dorcas hesitates and adds, "I honestly didn't know that's how I felt until I said it."

"Hey, Dorcas, change your life if you want to—I'm all for that—but don't blame it on your mother. Even if you think an eighty-year-old painting naked guys is 'completely normal.'"

Dorcas drops back against the sofa cushions, unsure again. "You're right," she sighs. For a while, neither says a word.

"What about Alex?" Rootie asks suddenly. "Do you have any contact with him?"

"Alex? Lavinia asked me the same thing. I steer clear except when I have to act as a referee between him and Sasha."

"I thought Sasha was the apple of his eye."

"She was. But when she outgrew her role as Perfect Daughter, she fell from grace. She pisses him off, he disowns her, she feels guilty, I intervene, he forgives her, they make up, I'm out of the picture until she does something else."

The sherry is gone. Rootie rummages in the pantry and finds a dusty bottle of rum and decides to make tea to pour it into. They stand in the kitchen, waiting for the water to boil. "Has Sasha found another guy?"

"If she has, she hasn't told me."

"Is she planning to stay in California?" Rootie pours hot water over teabags in chipped mugs.

"Apparently. She claims to love it out there." Dorcas speaks lightly, as if it doesn't matter much. "Maybe the reason Sasha and I get along so well is because we live so far apart." Dorcas cradles the mug in both hands to warm them.

"That's something *you* might keep in mind." Rootie lights another cigarette. "So what are you going to do if your offer's accepted?"

"Oh, that's simple!" Dorcas ticks them off, hearing little ripples of mania in her own voice: "Quit my hopeless job, dump my hopeless non-lover, sell the townhouse, turn the derelict William Alfred Morgan House into a bed-and-breakfast, keep an eye on my sex-crazed mother, and find true happiness in the last decade of the twentieth century." Dorcas buries her face in her hands.

"Hey look, nobody'd be happier than me if you moved back. We'll have a ball! But you've got to think about it seriously."

"I *have* thought about it seriously," Dorcas says grumpily. They carry their fortified tea into the living room.

"I mean for more than just one day."

"You sound like my mother."

Rootie puffs her cheeks and blows. "Getting back to Lavinia—have you talked to her about the paintings?"

Dorcas concentrates on the split in the upholstery of Rootie's couch. It has become a large hole. "I've seen them, but she doesn't know that yet. They're locked up in a secret closet. And I have no idea who Nicholas is."

"Are you going to ask her?"

"I don't know. Maybe. Someday. Is there any more rum?"

"A drop. I'll make some more tea."

"Don't bother. All I want is the rum." She's already had too much. The rum sloshes in her mug. "Listen, Rootie," she says, "if all the men I've ever been involved with were laid end to end, they would go exactly nowhere. I'd still be fifty-four and alone, with a job I stopped enjoying a long time ago. And that's why I want to buy that derelict house and change my life. Does that make any sense?"

"I'll drink to it," Rootie says, and they do.

Again Dorcas tosses restlessly on the sofa bed—she can feel every spring—but tonight she's thinking about the house. She progresses through the upstairs rooms, picturing each one decorated in a different style and named after a flower: the Daisy Room, all in yellow, the Lilac Room in shades of purple, the Lily of the Valley Room, white with touches of green.

Then she thinks about money. Buying Morgan House is not a problem; fixing it up is the problem. She has no idea how much renovations would cost. Around three A.M. she turns on the light and begins working out a financial plan on the back of an envelope: cash in her CDs for the down payment, take out a mortgage for the rest; sell the townhouse and use the proceeds for the remodeling. Her savings, plus whatever she can earn subbing in the Juniata schools, if she has to, should give her enough to live on until the B&B is up and running. It could work. It *will* work.

She turns off the light again. Still she can't sleep. *Jimmy O'Brien.* Jimmy already knew he was going to be a priest when he took her to the all-night party after the prom and begged her to have sex with him just once so he'd know what he was giving up. "It would not be a sin under these circumstances," he'd argued. "More like an act of charity." Of course she said no; she was too scared.

She climbs out of bed as soon as it's light outside. Lavinia is in the bathroom. Dorcas uses the toilet in the tiny powder room and takes off for a walk, rushing straight to Morgan House. This time she walks around to the old stable. Somebody had once tried to fix it up and then abandoned the idea; it's filled with junk. Nothing she sees changes her mind.

The moment Dorcas returns, Lavinia begins to fix a pot of oatmeal. "I wondered where you got to."

"I went by that old house again. I guess that slowed me down some." *Tell her. Tell her.* She clears her throat. "Mother, I've decided to make an offer on the place." Lavinia stares at her, wooden spoon arrested in space. "I want to buy it."

Lavinia sits down suddenly. "You can't be serious, Dorcas. Why would you want to buy an old wreck like that? And what are you intending to do with it? Not live in it, surely."

"I'll fix it up. I'm thinking of turning it into a bed-and-breakfast. You know, a guest house, sort of." Dorcas says this offhandedly, as though there's nothing to it.

"Bed-and-breakfast! You've lost your mind! Have you any idea what it would cost to make that place habitable? Do you even know what it takes to run a bed-and-breakfast?"

Lavinia's blue eyes are like lasers. "I can't imagine who'd ever want to stay there," she continues relentlessly. "This isn't a tourist town. If some traveling salesman has to spend the night, he'll stay out at Mountain View Motel. And just what are you intending to live on in the meantime? I plan to leave you some money someday, Dorcas, but not *yet!*"

Each of her mother's small, sensible arrows flies straight to the target. Stung, Dorcas holds up her hand for a truce. "Let me take my shower and get dressed, and we can talk about it."

Under the soothing stream of hot water, Dorcas weeps. What had she expected from Lavinia? Applause? Dorcas knows better. When she comes out in jeans and a woolen sweater, her mother is dishing up the oatmeal. "Your eyes are puffy," Lavinia remarks.

"Shampoo."

"You'd better eat this before it dries out," Lavinia says, briskly setting a bowl of cereal at Dorcas's place. "Do they serve oatmeal at those places? That's what I'd want if I were to stay at a bed-and-breakfast. Oatmeal and raisin toast and fresh orange juice. Make sure the mattresses are good. Everybody wants a nice firm bed. Also decent towels. Thick."

"Oh, I would," Dorcas agrees, reaching for the milk.

"What are they asking for it?"

"Eighty-nine five."

"Eighty-nine five! They're lucky if they get half that. Offer fifty. That's being generous."

"I was thinking sixty-five."

"Hah," Lavinia snorts. "I still think you're nuts."

"I know."

"You'll lose your shirt. But nobody can tell you anything, Dorcas. You always have to find out the hard way."

Dorcas makes an eleven o'clock appointment with Sharon to put in an offer. As she hurries down the stairs, Lavinia calls after her, "Remember, Dorcas, bid low! Not a penny over fifty!"

CHAPTER 6

Dorcas proposes a Saturday afternoon drive. They roll out Lavinia's ancient Lincoln Continental, in mint condition with less than thirty thousand miles. "I don't drive much anymore," Lavinia says, settling into the creamy leather seat. "But I can't bear the idea of getting rid of it."

Dorcas is dying to go past Morgan House but decides not to, since it would just trigger another barrage of criticism. Instead, they go to the cemetery where Dorcas learned to drive. Lavinia brought her here to practice on the narrow, winding lanes, but they always ended up yelling at each other; Lavinia announced that she was through, finished, done, and if anybody was going to teach Dorcas to drive, it would have to be Edgar, which is what Dorcas had wanted all along. Her father never lost patience, and once she got her license, Edgar let her have the car whenever she asked for it.

Among a field of modest granite tablets of pink or gray, a gleaming white marble arch frames an urn. The arch is flanked by two slabs topped with classic finials. The slab to the right is incised with the names and dates of Lavinia's parents, Clarence and Edna Y. Miller, and Lavinia's un-married sister, Sarah, always called Sister. On the other slab is Dorcas's father's name, Edgar F. Buchanan, 1901–1962, and beneath it, Lavinia Miller Buchanan, 1910–. The sight of their names gives Dorcas a painful twinge.

"I like to come out here once in a while," Lavinia says, "just to make sure nobody's filled in my date."

While Lavinia fusses with the pots of lilies they've brought from the florist, Dorcas wanders among the tomb-stones, reading the carved names, Millers and Buchanans, and a sad cluster of small stones with the names of children.

They leave the cemetery and drive past Dorcas's old grade school, yellow brick with a cavernous entry, long ago converted to county offices, and then on to the Mountain View Motel, built on land that had once been part of Clarence Miller's farm. The year Lavinia was born, Clarence founded Juniata Marble and Granite. When she entered high school, Clarence turned the operation of the farm over to his brother and moved his wife and daughters to town.

"Crying shame, how they tore down our old farmhouse," Lavinia says as they cruise through the motel parking lot. "Much better than that mess you've got your heart set on. I've been wondering—are you having another midlife cri-sis, Dorcas? Because there ought to be a cheaper way to do it this time."

The last time, Dorcas knows, marveling at her mother's ability to come up with such barbs, was divorcing Alex. Lavinia always considered Alex an oddball—his strange foreign ways put her off—but once Dorcas had divorced him, he acquired new status. He became *poor Alex.*

"Why 'poor Alex,' Mother?" Dorcas demanded. He'd come out of the marriage almost intact financially; it had taken Dorcas five years to pay off her legal bills.

"You wounded his pride. That's very hard on a man, you know," Lavinia explained.

"He'll get over it." And he did—much sooner than Dorcas herself.

She decides to ignore Lavinia's latest crack. "I haven't bought it yet," she says. "I made a really low offer, sixty-three five, because I know it's going to cost a fortune to fix it up."

"An arm and a leg," Lavinia agrees. "A king's ransom."

"And there's a good chance the owners will turn it down. So I don't really have my hopes up too high." A lie—she has begun to feel as though her life depends on it.

Dorcas steers the Lincoln into a restaurant parking lot. "We might as well stop at Rocco's for dinner, as long as we're at this end of town, don't you think? Unless there's something else you'd rather do?"

"Suits me," Lavinia says amiably. "We're in time for the Early Bird Special."

Rocco's Ristorante Italiano, once owned by parents of a high school classmate, had been a hangout for Dorcas and her friends. The present owners kept the name and the red-and-white sign on the roof. Inside, the same neon *Schlitz* flickers on the wall; the same plastic ivy, velvety with dust, climbs a wooden trellis; the jukebox is gone, and tables cover the floor where Dorcas used to dance with Jimmy. The vinyl bench seats make farting sounds when Dorcas and Lavinia sit on them. A stuffed silver marlin has been leaping out of an imaginary ocean behind the bar for over forty years. *Can that possibly be the same fish*, Dorcas wonders, *or did somebody catch a new one?*

Dorcas orders a glass of red wine. Lavinia decides that a splash of Jack Daniels on the rocks won't hurt her. Before their drinks arrive, Dorcas finds the pay phone by the rest rooms, calls Sharon Dieter, and gets her answering machine.

Lavinia looks up expectantly when Dorcas returns. "No news," Dorcas reports.

"Patience has never been one of your virtues," her mother reminds her.

The waitress, grinning familiarly at Lavinia, sets little plastic bowls of shredded lettuce in front of them. Lavinia is talking about church again, wondering out loud what the choir director has planned for music at the Easter service tomorrow. "Esther Reed doesn't know *beans* about church music," Lavinia laments. "Never did know how to direct, lost her voice years ago, and doesn't have the good sense to quit. The choir is just a disaster. I'm so glad I'm not involved anymore."

Dorcas, listening absentmindedly, knows what that means: Lavinia secretly wishes she were still running the show.

The plates arrive—pasta soft as wet soap, meatballs that would bounce if dropped. "Mother," Dorcas asks suddenly, "were you ever in love with anybody besides Daddy?"

Lavinia's blue eyes gleam. She pats her mouth with her napkin. "Dozens," she says coyly. "I had dozens of beaux." She smiles and spreads margarine on a roll.

Dorcas smiles back. "I mean, anybody in particular. A great love. A grand passion." She gestures theatrically.

Lavinia appears to consider the question deeply. "No," she says. "I don't think so. Just your father." Another smile; she's quite an actress, really. "But I've gotten so old, Dorcas, that I can hardly remember anymore."

When Dorcas was in her early teens, she loved to page through Lavinia's yearbook from 1928 and scrapbooks filled with newspaper clippings, dance cards, recital programs. In her youth, Lavinia had attracted plenty of attention with her good looks and her clear singing voice. Dorcas grew up hearing stories from her aunt about Lavinia's suitors. But no mention of Nicholas.

The owner of a shoe store, the nice-looking engineer for Bell Telephone, and the manager of the bank where Clarence Miller did business were all considered desirable matches, but it was Edgar Buchanan she finally agreed to marry. Edgar worked for Lavinia's father as foreman of the monument company, and, according to Sister, he was hand-picked by Clarence to marry Lavinia. She was willing because Edgar danced so well—that was the way the story went.

When Dorcas was young, she couldn't imagine her mother marrying somebody just because Clarence picked him for her. Dorcas thinks of her parents' wedding picture, a snapshot taken in 1933 in her grandparents' backyard, Lavinia's arm looped through Edgar's, her white straw hat at a jaunty tilt, a gardenia pinned to the shoulder of her crepe dress with wide, fluttery sleeves. In the photograph she's laughing. Next to her, Sister wears a tight little smile, hands curled into fists at her sides. Sister, the old maid. Dorcas used to wonder if her aunt was jealous of Lavinia. How could she not have been? If Sister knew about Lavinia's secret passion, she had not told Dorcas, never even hinted there might have been one. Sister has been dead for years. There's no one left now for Dorcas to ask, except Lavinia.

❧

During the long Easter morning service Dorcas glances at her mother beside her in the pew, smartly dressed in her lavender wool tweed suit and pearls, faintly yellowed kid-skin gloves. Dorcas thinks of the woman-statue in the painting, head thrown back, mouth open: Lavinia in ecstasy. A tiny nerve begins to pulse in Dorcas's eyelid; she presses her finger against it.

Later they put in a call to Sasha. No one answers, and Dorcas leaves a silly message on the machine from the Easter Bunny.

And then, while they're eating the ham crusted with brown sugar and cloves, Sharon Dieter calls. The offer on Morgan House has been accepted. Hands shaking, Dorcas reports the news to her mother.

"They didn't haggle? Try to get more?"

"Nope." Dorcas sits down heavily, her knees weak.

"Well, that just goes to show you how anxious they are to dump it. You should have offered less. Fifty would have been plenty."

Dorcas bites her tongue. She was thinking the same thing.

Lavinia sighs and lifts her water glass. "Well, good luck, Dorcas," she says. "You're certainly going to need it."

CHAPTER 7

Gus forks steamers into a cup of clam broth and nests the empty clamshells, one inside the other, around the rim of his plate. Dorcas has observed him eating artichokes in this same meticulous manner, arranging the leaves in a semicircle. He bites corn off the cob in clean, even rows. Watching him now, Dorcas slings her clamshells carelessly, letting them fall on the polished tabletop.

Barbara Lambert had pointed him out several years ago at a fund-raiser for one of her clients: "He's the administrator at the hospital. Not bad, huh?" Dorcas *had* liked his looks—pewter-colored hair, neatly trimmed mustache, amused gray eyes, glasses.

The next weekend he invited her to a jazz concert. Dorcas had once seen Louis Armstrong in person, and Edgar liked Duke Ellington. This seemed like a good start. They had a drink afterward and debated assisted suicide, women in the military, gays in the military, capital punishment, abortion, the legalization of pot, school uniforms, coming down on opposite sides of every issue but school uniforms—they both liked that idea.

Barbara phoned the following Wednesday. "You probably don't want to hear this, but here's what I found out: Gus's wife ran off with the minister at their church and left their three boys with him. This was years ago. Two of the boys are gone, one's still at home. It was a huge scandal. He's still gun-shy. So take it easy."

"Oh, I will." She meant it, too.

Gus showed up three days later with a bunch of daffodils and a bad head cold. "I probably shouldn't have come," he said apologetically. "But I wanted to see you."

He reached out, tentatively placed his hand on her shoulder, and let it rest there. With one finger he gently stroked the little hollow at the base of her skull. Dorcas felt the warmth start at her knees and move up to meet the fingers now buried in her hair. He drew her onto his lap, her head on his shoulder, his fingers circling her ears and then, pulling up her sweater, her nipples. She moved, awkwardly, toward his mouth.

"You'll catch my cold," he murmured.

"I take a lot of vitamin C."

"Dorcas," he said, "I want very much to take you to bed, but I don't know where the bedroom is."

Already aroused, she led him to the bedroom, wanting him to come into her quickly, just the unzipped fly, the lifted skirt, the pantyhose peeled away. But Gus proceeded so deliberately, taking such care to hang his pants over the back of the chair, his shirt draped over it with his glasses safely in the pocket, that her ardor began to cool. When at last he eased inside her, the results were disappointing. *Maybe later*, she thought; they could have lunch, have some coffee, come back to bed.

But when they'd eaten the reheated soup and a peach tart, Gus had to leave; his fifteen-year-old son, Gary, was at home alone.

Early on, Gus gave her a pet name: Ducks.

At first it seemed sweet and wonderful, an endearment. And she'd been delighted with the little gifts he gave her, all with a duck theme: a box of yellow duck soap; a duck-shaped teapot; paper cocktail napkins and a doormat with duck designs; and, on their first Christmas together, a handsome woodcut of mallards swimming among cattails. But then Dorcas realized that Gus had started using the name whenever she'd done something he didn't approve of, like the incident with the panties.

She had invited him to spend Sunday afternoon, beginning with brunch. After they'd finished the mimosas and made love, she put on the lacy new bra and panties bought for the occasion, making sure she had Gus's attention. Gus sat on the edge of the bed, a brown sock dangling from each hand.

He cleared his throat. "Ducks, I'm going to be frank—I don't think it's appropriate for a woman your age to wear bikini underpants."

Dorcas, balanced storklike with one leg through the panty leghole, thought he was kidding. Of course he was kidding! Keeping up her end of the joke, she launched into a burlesque routine, bumping and grinding and kicking the wisp of ivory lace and satin into the air and then unhooking the bra and twirling it in figure-eights before she took a second look at Gus's stony face.

"Inappropriate? What do you mean, 'inappropriate'?"

"I mean, I'd like you better in something more modest."

She yanked on the panties that had drifted to the floor like jellyfish. "Something from a religious supply house?" she screeched. "With Mother Teresa embroidered on it instead of Christian Dior?"

She told Barbara the story, omitting that she'd gone out and bought a half dozen plain white briefs and stuffed the bikinis in the back of her underwear drawer.

During the course of her relationship with Gus, Gary had gotten older and presumably less innocent, but everything between Gus and Dorcas stayed the same: all right as long as she maintained a safe distance, made no demands. But three-plus years into it, when she'd all but given up, he'd said, "Honey, I think we ought to get married." And she'd taken that as a commitment, called Barbara, called Lavinia and Sasha, crowed the happy news to Dr. Wellborn, started making plans. Then he withdrew the offer in Florida. Bastard! Since January they've treated each other with elaborate care, as though the other were terminally ill.

⚜

The waiter clears away the clamshells. Dorcas has been back from Juniata for two days, and they've met for dinner at The Captain's Table, a seafood restaurant near Long Island Sound. Dorcas has come in her own car.

"How is Lavinia?" Gus asks. He met her once, and they'd striven to outdo each other in the charm department.

"Actually she's in fine fettle. I hope I'm in as good shape as she is when I'm her age."

"What about her paintings? Are they really shocking?"

"Depends what you consider shocking, but they *are* erotic—my friend Rootie was right about that. They're also very good. I have no idea who the naked man is that she's presented in a full frontal view. All I know is it's not my father."

The waiter brings their broiled fish. When he asks if they'd like anything else, Gus shakes his head, but Dorcas orders a second glass of wine, grimly noting Gus's slight frown. The wine arrives; she takes a deep breath and raises her glass.

"I would like you to join me in a toast to my new enterprise: Morgan House," she begins nervously. Her hand is trembling.

Gus picks up his carefully hoarded half glass. "All right. But first tell me what that is."

"Morgan House is a beautiful old mansion in Juniata. I discovered it over the weekend and decided to buy it for a bed-and-breakfast. I plan to move back there within the next couple of months." Courage is draining out of her like blood from a severed artery, but Dorcas manages a shaky smile. She gulps more wine.

"Ducks, have you lost your mind?"

There it is again: the shocked disapproval. "No, Gus," she says, "I think I've just found it. And please call me Dorcas." That feels better; she's stanched the hemorrhage.

Gus sets down his glass. "You've thought this through carefully, I suppose," he says.

Dorcas tosses down a third of her second glass of wine. "It's time for me to change my life," she continues recklessly, "do something different, get away from the kids at school. Teaching is eating me alive."

She pokes at her shad. If she expected Gus to take her face in his two hands and say, "Don't go, Dorcas, I can't live without you," that expectation is doomed. It always has been.

She can't bear to stay another moment; the danger of weakening always lurks when she's with Gus. She opens her purse and drops a ten and a twenty on the table. "My share of the tab," she says, shoving back her chair. "I'll send you an invitation to the opening."

CHAPTER 8

Rodney Benner is a big man who moves with care, as though afraid of bumping into something fragile and breaking it. His high school crew cut is now gray stubble, a wheat field in November. The freckles have faded but the grin is the same, down to the chipped tooth the girls used to think was so cute.

It was Lavinia's idea to hire Rod. "Just look at my apartment," Lavinia said, and Dorcas saw that she was right: his attentive workmanship spoke for itself.

On the Saturday after she recklessly agreed to buy Morgan House, she has driven back to Juniata and walks through the house with Rodney, making notes on a yellow legal pad. They start at the roof and work their way down to the basement, and Rod talks her through the list of what needs to be done.

Rod has a helper for the drywall work and subcontracts the plumbing and electrical. He'll take care of the carpentry and the floors himself. They'll need to hire a mason to point up the exterior brick and check the chimneys;

a furnace man, a roofer who can work with slate, a sheet metal guy to replace gutters and downspouts. She writes it all down.

She should have done this before she got in so deep, signed the contract and handed over a thousand dollars to an escrow account. Legally she can still get out of it— sacrifice the earnest money and run. *That might be the smart thing to do,* she thinks as the list grows longer and her panic rises; *it isn't too late yet.* As she sketches room by room, windows and doors, noting dimensions as Rod measures them off, imagining how it will look when it's done, she notices she's developing a rash on her hands. Her stomach hurts. Rod whistles softly through his teeth and gets on her nerves.

It's noon when they complete the survey of the house. "We could get some lunch at the Trolley Stop," Rod says in the matter-of-fact way she remembers.

The waitress wears a picture of a teenage boy laminated in a plastic badge on the bosom of her brown uniform. She grins at Dorcas and winks at Rod.

"Did she go to school with us?" Dorcas whispers when the waitress leaves.

"Naah. I'm not sure Wanda finished school. Her boy that died, the one in the picture she's wearing? He was a real shit, excuse my French. Drugs and all."

"My mother says Wanda's had a very hard life. Lavinia comes here a lot." Dorcas knows that if she ever told her mother the kinds of tales Wanda regularly confides to Lavinia—losing at bingo, hooking up with men who drink, maxing out her credit cards—Lavinia's response would be censure, not sympathy.

"I know. I come here a lot too, since Marlene and I split. You knew we were split?"

Dorcas nods.

Wanda bustles in, skimming the booths with her hip, and plunks down two cups. Coffee slops into the saucers. "Hear you're moving back to town, Dorcas," she says. From her apron pocket she produces bundles of silverware wrapped in paper napkins.

"Yes," Dorcas says, forcing a smile. "I'm pretty excited." *Terrified* is more accurate. She begins to arrange the silverware, fork on the left, knife and spoon on the right. The way Lavinia would.

"So's your mom," Wanda reports. "If it was me, I'd a been back here a long time ago." She laughs, a rasp that ends in a cough. "But then, I never left, so what does that tell you?" She winks again at Rod and heads for the kitchen.

"What do you think?" Dorcas asks. "About the house."

"The honest truth? I think you bought yourself a great old house and a whole lot of work." He stirs three packets of sugar into his coffee.

"I bought a dream," Dorcas explains.

"Dreams don't come cheap."

"How much?" The coffee isn't hot, but she sips it carefully, as if it were. "Off the top of your head?"

"Too early to say. I don't do top of the head, and I don't do ballpark. There's still a lot for you to decide. How many bathrooms you want. The layout of the kitchen, since you're going to serve food. That kind of thing. And you never know what you're getting into with an old house," he says. "Figure out what you think the job is worth, and double it. Then triple it, to be on the safe side. It's none of my business, Dorcas, but is money going to be a problem?"

Dorcas explains her plan: cashing in her savings, getting a mortgage, selling her townhouse.

Rod pulls out a thick, yellow carpenter's pencil and sketches a couple of kitchen designs on Dorcas's legal pad. Dorcas watches his hands. He has long, tapering fingers, more like a pianist's than a carpenter's. No wedding ring, but the pale ghost of one.

When Dorcas came back to Juniata for her twenty-fifth high school reunion, the year she and Alex were divorced, Rod and Marlene were awarded the prize for "Most Romantic Couple."

"So where do we start?" she asks. She taps the legal pad, five pages covered with notes and Rod's little drawings.

"By cleaning the place out. I'll put Charlie to work on that. You know my nephew, Charlie? Hard worker. He does odd jobs for your mother—you can ask her. Next thing is the roof and the windows. We get started soon as the place is yours. When's the closing?"

"That depends on the bank."

"I'll lean on the loan officer. Steve Gutshall—his dad taught chemistry, remember? Smoky Gutshall? I'll show Steve our plans, get him to move things along."

Dorcas has forgotten how everybody in Juniata is related somehow.

Wanda brings her tuna on rye, his meatloaf and fries, and leaves the check, folded like a tent. Rod reaches for it, ignoring Dorcas's protests.

He turns on the Rod Benner chipped-tooth grin as they shake hands outside. "Welcome back, Dorcas," he says. "It'll be good to have you here. We'll make you a beautiful home. You'll see."

⁂

When the bank opens Monday morning, Dorcas is there. Steve Gutshall and Sharon steer her through the paperwork. After she stops to say good-bye to Lavinia, who asks too many questions that Dorcas can't answer, she leaves for Connecticut. She spends the evening typing out her letter of resignation.

It's still not too late, she reminds herself. The rash on her hands is worse.

The next night, Tuesday, Dorcas brews a mug of Earl Grey and calls Sasha in California. It's the one night she knows that Sasha isn't at work at the restaurant she manages or taking a class. Her daughter's hectic schedule worries Dorcas.

She pictures Sasha, slender, with small, delicate features, her dark brown hair cut short, or maybe she's let it grow again. Whichever it is, she'll be fiddling with it, twisting it around her finger if it's long enough, raking her fingers through it if it's short, unable to leave it alone. Her eyes are dark and intense, the only brown eyes in the family, and her thick lashes and wide brows are black as charcoal. Sasha has always been proud of her eyes. Mysterious, she says—unfathomable.

What Sasha says when Dorcas tells her about her plans for Morgan House is, "Are you having a midlife crisis, Mom?"

"That's what your grandmother asked," Dorcas replies stonily. "Lovey's exact words. May I remind you that I'm too old for a midlife crisis? The time for that was ten years ago."

"Then it must be senile dementia. Should I be making plans to institutionalize you?"

Dorcas doesn't like this joke. "Why do you see this in such negative terms? Think of it as a romantic fling, a substitute for sex in my golden years."

Sasha laughs. Dorcas loves the sound of her laugh. As a child Sasha seemed to be laughing all the time, but there was a period, during her teens, when the laughter was stifled. Dorcas blamed herself for that, which is probably exactly what Sasha intended. "So you're finally done with that wimpy shit."

An image of Gus flickers briefly. Dorcas wills it to pass. "I'm off men, period. Probably for good."

"Mother, please. You've never been off men in your entire life!"

"Sasha, for God's sake!" She's a little offended. "I didn't call you to discuss my love life. I called to tell you about this wonderful old house which you will fall in love with the minute you see it."

"What does Lovey think? Is she in love with it, too?"

Dorcas hesitates. "To be honest, no. She thinks it's a wreck, and it does need a lot of work, I admit that. But I see it as a way to start my life over. Reinvent myself, as they say." She takes a long swallow of tea and notices that she's picked the mug with a parade of yellow ducks on it. "And, if you want to talk about love lives, how's yours? Are you dating anybody interesting?"

She has sworn ever since Sasha's teenage marriage fell apart before it had scarcely begun that she would never ask her daughter that kind of question, exactly the kind Lavinia would ask. She can anticipate Sasha's answer: a flat *no*, without the rising wistful note that would indicate she was even looking.

"I'll pretend I didn't hear that question." Sasha's voice comes across thousands of miles of the North American landmass and light years of unexplored mother-daughter space.

"Okay—I'll pretend I didn't ask it." Dorcas thinks of Lavinia's barbed comment, *You're different from me. You need a man.* It occurs to her that Sasha is like Lavinia. Something to do with alternate generations.

"You're actually going to move back to Juniata? I can't believe you'd do that. I thought you hated Juniata. You always told Dad it was a hick town. You always said you couldn't wait to get away. You and Lovey still argue over what clothes you should wear. Do you even have any friends there anymore?"

"Rootie," Dorcas says.

"Who?"

"Ruth Kauffman. And a guy from our old crowd is doing the remodeling, and his ex-wife who's Lovey's hairdresser. And there's lots of new people in town. They move there from Philadelphia and Pittsburgh because it's small and rural, you know, and safe. So I'll make new friends." The tea she brewed is too strong; she wishes she'd put in some lemon. "There's another reason I'm doing this," Dorcas adds. "For Lovey."

"She isn't sick or anything, is she?"

"Physically, she's seems solid as a rock. But I worry some about her mental state. She's as sharp as ever, but she's been doing these paintings." Dorcas describes the nude paintings and the reaction of the town.

"Cool!" says Sasha.

"Cool?" Dorcas echoes. "Sasha, people are really upset about this. It's as though she deliberately set out to shock everyone. I want to read you what they wrote in the paper."

The article in the *Philadelphia Inquirer* of March 16, 1991, had treated the paintings unsensationally, mentioned as part of a series the newspaper did on creative octogenarians. Lavinia immediately picked up on the writer's patronizing attitude. "It's the art that's important, not my age!" she grumbled, but nevertheless seemed pleased. The Harrisburg paper, though, played up the reaction of the community to the "shocking" paintings, which the art critic, quoted in a sidebar, described as "elegantly rendered" with "fine draftsmanship."

"And this is why you're moving to Juniata?" Sasha asks scornfully. "To get Lovey to put fig leaves on her nudes?"

"There's a lot more to it than that."

"Mother," Sasha says patiently, "I give it two years. Three, max. I don't see how you're going to make any money with a B&B. Juniata isn't exactly Santa Cruz."

And on and on. Sasha *is* like Lavinia. Dorcas studies the tea mug. The ducks wear little red rubber boots and carry umbrellas as they march around the mug in single file, except for one duck marching in the opposite direction. Gus gave it to her for Easter last year with a bunch of daisies stuck in it.

"That's you, Dorcas," he'd said. "A duck with a mind of her own."

For a moment Dorcas misses Gus so intensely that her throat clamps shut.

"It's going to work, Sasha," says Dorcas, when she can talk again. "The big question is, when are you coming to see it?"

"Soon," Sasha says vaguely. "Maybe at the end of the summer. I've been thinking I ought to see Daddy."

"Oh, are you two speaking again?"

"It's not that we're not speaking, it's that we don't speak. Ellen calls sometimes, so at least I know he's alive."

After she hangs up, Dorcas remembers that she forgot to say anything about the overdue thank-you note to Lavinia.

❦

Barbara flings open the door the moment Dorcas rings the bell. A strapping woman with hazel eyes and bountiful breasts that Dorcas has always envied, she pushes Dorcas onto the dove gray suede sofa. "Now bring me up-to-date," she commands.

There's a lot to cover: first, Lavinia's paintings of Nicholas, and then Morgan House. Dorcas describes it the way she envisions it, not the way it is; to be honest is to admit the insanity of what she's done.

"Ohmigod!" Barbara moans and rakes her manicured fingers through her highlighted hair. "You bought a place out in the middle of nowhere just like *that?*"

"It's not the middle of nowhere."

"Well, I promise you this: Harold and I will be out to see you as soon as Morgan House opens," Barbara declares. "You've hired an architect to oversee the renovations, right?"

Dorcas shakes her head.

Barbara frowns. "But a good contractor, surely? You've worked out what needs to be done, what it's going to cost to do it all? *No?* Jesus, Dorcas!" She leans forward, eyes narrowed. "Listen, it's none of my business, but have you figured out the finances for all of this? Because I could, you know, make you a loan if you need it."

Dorcas tries to protest, but Barbara waves her off. "No, no, just shut up and listen. It would be strictly a business deal. It's better than struggling along for years on a frayed shoestring, isn't it?"

"Thanks," Dorcas says. Barbara always talks about money so much more frankly than she ever could. "I really appreciate it. But I can't do that. It'll work out fine." She doesn't feel nearly as confident as she sounds.

Barbara shrugs, and her marvelous breasts pitch up and down. "Whatever you say. But you know if you ever get in a pinch, I'm here, checkbook in hand. What's the point of being rich, if you can't help out a friend? I think this calls for a toast."

Barbara produces a bottle of champagne and pours it into crystal flutes. They sit with their feet propped on the rosewood coffee table. "To your adventure," Barbara says, raising her glass.

The bubbles moving swiftly through her veins convince Dorcas that she's doing the right thing. Her confidence swells. She feels good.

Barbara tops off the crystal flutes. "Dorcas," she says, "we've been friends forever, right?"

"Twenty-five years," Dorcas agrees fondly. She's getting a little nostalgic, thinking about how their lives have changed. "I was pregnant with Sasha when we moved to the house behind yours. Your twins were just babies. You were nursing them. Remember?"

"Yeah." Barbara smiles and hitches around so that her hazel eyes gaze straight into Dorcas's blue ones. "I've been looking at you ever since you walked in here tonight, and I have to tell you something, Dorcas: you are the perfect candidate for a face-lift."

Dorcas flinches. "Face-lift?"

"Well, sure! I got one about five years ago, around the time I started dating Harold. I decided I needed an edge, you know? There are a zillion women out there looking for men, and to be honest, I was on the high end, age-wise, and men in our age group are all looking for younger women. Sixty-year-old farts dating girls the age of our daughters!"

Dorcas sips her champagne, pondering what she imagines was intended as a compliment.

"Dorcas," Barbara continues earnestly, "can I be honest? Think about your hair. You should color it. Men don't like gray hair on women. It reminds them of their mothers. It reminds them of their own mortality. Of *death*, Dorcas! Men can't handle that."

"I like my face," Dorcas mutters.

"Well, sure you do! And you do have beautiful eyes. It was just a suggestion."

Dorcas fakes a yawn, eager now to get away. "I've got to be going. Say hello to Harold for me, will you?"

Later, at home, Dorcas stands in front of the bathroom mirror and pinches up tiny folds of flesh around her ears and chin, trying to imagine what it might be like to look thirty again.

CHAPTER 9

The day after Mother's Day, Morgan House is hers.

On weekend visits, Lavinia treats her as though she were sixteen—old enough to drive but not to be trusted. To get Rod's work started, Dorcas has asked her mother for a loan to tide her over until her townhouse sells; the notion of taking Barbara up on her offer to help is too awkward, even though it would not be accompanied by a lecture. Lavinia can't seem to refrain from reminding Dorcas about fiscal responsibility.

Her mother also announces that her friend Stella McAllister is moving to a senior apartment at Coleman House. "About time, too, because between you and me and the fence post, she's losing it," Lavinia reports. "She's going to have an auction. So I said to her, 'Stella, you know that auctioneer is probably crooked as a dog's hind leg. He'll take a big percentage and tell you the rest is worthless, and then he'll haul it all down to Philadelphia and sell it to dealers for a huge profit.'

"And then when I had her attention, which isn't easy, poor thing, I said, 'You know Dorcas is opening a bed-and-breakfast, and she might be able to give you a fair dollar for some of that stuff you want to get rid of.' I told her we'd be over in the morning."

As they park in front of Mrs. McAllister's house, Lavinia grips Dorcas's arm hard and whispers, "Now you signal me when you're interested in something, but let me do the talking."

They pick out a walnut gate-leg table and eight cane-bottom chairs, a drop-leaf serving table in cherry, two mahogany chests of drawers, a pine dry-sink, a set of old china, and a magnificent corner cupboard with twelve panes of the original rippled, bubbly glass. They dicker a little; Stella turns stubborn. "I've had an appraiser in here, Lavinia," Stella says. "I know what things are worth."

Lavinia gets out her checkbook. "They're worth only what somebody is willing to pay for them—I learned that with my paintings. Remember, Stella, a fast nickel beats a slow dime. I'm offering you cash on the barrelhead. This doesn't happen every day." Dorcas gazes out the window, embarrassed. Her mother is much tougher than she is.

Dorcas and Lavinia head for the Trolley Stop. When they've given Wanda their order for the lunch special, hot turkey sandwiches, Lavinia asks, "By the way—what does Sasha have to say about all this?"

Dorcas shrugs. "She thinks I'm out of my mind."

"Sensible girl," Lavinia says. "When you talk to her again, remind her for me that I still haven't gotten that thank-you note. It's a good six weeks overdue."

❧

No matter how much Dorcas tells herself that she's doing something immensely positive for the first time in her life, she feels most of the time as though she's made of something insubstantial that could be easily crushed, melted, vaporized. She sleeps poorly, eats the wrong food, and drinks more than she should. She's tired most of the time.

On the last day of school the kids stage a farewell party and bring her a cake with her name misspelled. Aretha Jones's dark eyes glitter with tears, and she refuses to touch the cake.

"I'll write to you," Dorcas whispers. "We'll stay in touch. It will be okay." But she knows better.

Several times she cruises slowly past Gus's house. She imagines ringing his doorbell, pictures the look on his face when he opens the door and sees her standing there. Sometimes, in her fantasy, he looks delighted, as though he's been waiting for her. She doesn't stop. He doesn't call.

Her townhouse hasn't sold. Not so much as an offer.

⚜

Early in June she takes Rootie on a tour of Morgan House. The old carpet, filthy and matted as roadkill, has been ripped up and basic repair work begun—broken windowpanes and sash cords replaced, new slate on whole sections of the roof, new gutters installed. Now that school is out, Rod's nephew, Charlie, has been put to work scraping layers of paint from the bull's-eye molding around the windows and doors, revealing more cherry wood. Dorcas and Rootie leave footprints in the fine white powder that dusts the scarred floor.

"When are you moving in?" Rootie asks.

Dorcas ticks off all the things she has yet to do. "Maybe Labor Day," she says. "A lot of it's up to Rodney. He thinks I should keep the old cast-iron radiators and the ancient furnace. It still works, but we're putting in two new water heaters."

Rootie winks knowingly. "Still cute as a bug, isn't he?"

Sometimes Charlie goes out for sandwiches and the three of them—Charlie, Rod, and Dorcas—eat lunch in the old stable, where Rod has set up a workshop. Dorcas likes Charlie and someday, when the timing is right, she plans to ask him what *he* knows about Lavinia's paintings. He helped her hang them.

Mostly the lunch talk is about the house, but one day Rod said, "You know, I always wanted to teach history. That's why I enjoy working on these old places."

Dorcas looked up from her cole slaw, surprised. "I never knew that."

Days later, Dorcas balanced on a stepladder in the large east bedroom, stripping layers of wallpaper, sloshing liquid from a bucket onto the wall with a big sponge. Lavinia has loaned her an ancient radio that she keeps tuned to the oldies station. Mostly that means the 1970s, Beatles and Stones and other music that came after her era, but once in a while the deejay plunges all the way back to the pre-rock pop of the early 1950s. When he does, she sings along. That day she remembered most of the words: "Fly the ocean dee-dee-dah-dah-dah," she warbled, "See the jungle when it's dah-dee-dah."

Rod appeared in the doorway. "May I have this dance?"

She stared down at him from the ladder. "You mean now?"

"Come on, Dorcas. It was your class song. Remember?"

She climbed down, wiping her hands on her jeans. Strips of soggy wallpaper were piled on the floor like drifts of old snow. Her nose pressed against Rod's shoulder, his chin scratchy against her forehead, they danced. He smelled of fresh sweat, laundry soap, mineral spirits. Dorcas closed her eyes, swaying against him. When the music stopped, they stepped awkwardly away from each other.

That was two weeks ago. Since then Dorcas has moved around Rod cautiously, careful to stay outside his magnetic field. She senses that he's doing the same thing.

She thinks about that now and keeps a poker face in response to Rootie's grin. "Cute or not, he's doing a great job," Dorcas says. "That's all I care about."

"Oh, come on, Dorcas!" Rootie needles. "You can't kid me! Rod Benner has to be the best catch in town."

Rootie can't kid her, either. Dorcas understands at once that Rootie wants Rodney.

⁂

Toward the end of June, Dorcas begins teaching poetry and nature writing four days a week at a youth museum in Westport. Thursday afternoons she leaves for Juniata straight from the museum and spends two and a half days scraping paint off old doors and making decisions about light fixtures and hardware and what to do about the bathroom floor. Sunday afternoons she leaves late and fights traffic all the way back to Connecticut.

Barbara has been telling her that the townhouse will sell faster if she fixes it up. For two weekends Dorcas stays in Connecticut, painting the walls and woodwork plain white. Barbara spends an afternoon helping to pack away what she calls "distractions." Down comes the bulletin board with the hole-in-the-whole. Barbara hauls over a couple of tubs of flowers from one of her rental properties, to jazz up the entryway.

It works. Dorcas gets close to her asking price.

She calls a mover and begins to pack. This time she doesn't have to contend with Sasha.

After her divorce from Alex, Dorcas sold the house where Sasha grew up and moved to the townhouse. Sasha was furious, certain that Dorcas had driven Alex away. For weeks she refused to sleep in her new room and stayed with friends, two or three nights with one, then moving on to somebody else. It was Alex who finally brought Sasha home to Dorcas and talked her into staying. Not until Lavinia sold her house on Lindbergh Way did Dorcas really understand how Sasha must have felt—a part of her childhood taken away.

❧

To celebrate Dorcas's fifty-fifth birthday at the end of July as well as the sale of her townhouse, and as a going-away and good-luck gift, Barbara treats Dorcas to dinner at a country inn that boasts four stars from various dining guides.

"This is probably the last of your birthdays that you'll actually want to celebrate," Barbara says. "Starting now, you merely observe them with increasing wonder. Oh, Dorcas, how did we ever get to be so old and still feel so young?"

Dorcas has eaten at this restaurant once before, with Alex on their seventeenth wedding anniversary. Alex had picked that place and occasion to announce that his company, a manufacturer of car crash test dummies, was sending him to Detroit to oversee production at their new plant. "Is this permanent?" she asked, in a state of shock.

"Probably not. We're working on a new project, another type of dummy, and when it's ready to go on line, they'll want me back here."

Alex was excited, and to please him, Dorcas pretended to be as well, but she was unable to finish her meal.

She arranged for Sasha to stay with Barbara and dutifully flew to Detroit with Alex. The wife of the vice president took Dorcas to lunch and drove her around, pointing out which suburbs were desirable and which to stay away from. After dinner they attended a high school wrestling match to watch the vice president's son compete.

"If you had come next weekend," the wife said, "we could've gone down to hear the Detroit Symphony," and the vice president chuckled and said he was just as happy things worked out the way they did. "I'm not much on the long-hair stuff."

It was all wrong—the vice president, his wife, the suburbs, the wrestling match. Alex called her a snob; Dorcas said she didn't give a rat's ass where they lived since he spent every waking hour at work and they never saw him anyway.

In the end Dorcas and Sasha stayed in Connecticut and Alex rented an apartment in Detroit, coming home on weekends. That way, Dorcas explained to Lavinia, who thought the idea was outlandish, Sasha wouldn't have to change schools, Dorcas wouldn't have to look for a new job—she'd gone back to teaching when Sasha started first grade—and they wouldn't have to worry about what to do with their house.

At first, Alex flew home regularly, and then less often. Dorcas got used to having the bed to herself, to cooking when she felt like it. She was surprised at how little she missed him, although Sasha suffered from his absence. On the weekends that Alex stayed in Detroit, Dorcas and Barbara usually went out for dinner together, sometimes taking the girls along.

"You need to have an affair," Barbara said on one of the nights Sasha and the twins had gone to a friend's house for a sleepover.

"Great idea. Any suggestions?"

Barbara shook her head. "Unfortunately, no. If I did, I'd be on him myself in a minute. Incredible, all the guys who hung around like flies on a horse turd when I was married. Now that I'm single, I might as well be living in a convent."

"I'd be too scared," Dorcas admitted.

Barbara had that slightly loopy look that came with a third glass of wine. "You mean you never cheated on old Alex?"

"Once," Dorcas said. "That was enough."

"Oooh, tell me about it!" Barbara said with a leer. "You tell me about your affair, and I'll tell you about mine."

"Some other time," Dorcas said. But she never did.

Now Barbara turns off Route 7 onto a long driveway through an alley of poplars. She stops to put the top down on her red BMW, an anniversary present from Harold. "I hate convertibles," Barbara says, "except for making grand entrances."

Barbara orders Oysters Rockefeller and champagne. For the entrée they choose Truîte au Bleu, the trout to be plucked from a pond maintained by the chef and poached to order. They're in no hurry. "Think of this as an opera," the sleek waiter commands, presenting the oysters. "The curtain is now going up." He fills their glasses and discreetly disappears.

"So tell me," Barbara says. "How's it going? The remodeling and all?"

"Well, I'm not sure I can take all this trauma of starting over. But then I look at my mother. Lavinia has practically made a career of moving off in some new and totally unexpected direction without ever leaving home."

"I know you don't want to hear it," Barbara says, "but you're exactly like your mother."

From where she sits, Dorcas can see the table by the window where she sat opposite Alex on their anniversary so long ago, before she was forty, before her hair turned gray, before her marriage expired, before Sasha grew up and went away. The trout arrives, and waiters whisk out the fine filigree of bones. Their glasses are refilled. The opera goes on.

At the finale a team of waiters presents the dessert, a towering architectural marvel created from spun caramelized sugar. A violinist in a tuxedo appears at their table to play the first six notes of "Happy Birthday" in baroque style and then segues cleverly to something lively and sweet.

"You'll have to come out to Juniata for *your* birthday," Dorcas says, as they deconstruct the dessert. "It will be quietly perfect," she promises, "and perfectly elegant." This sounds good; she might use it in her brochure.

"That's in October, you know."

"The fifteenth. I remember." Dorcas watches as Barbara reapplies her lipstick and notices with a small surge of satisfaction that Barbara's face-lift seems to have odd little sags drooping here and there.

Then Barbara calls for vintage port for a final toast, and Dorcas slips almost painlessly into her middle fifties.

PART II

LAVINIA

CHAPTER 10

Lavinia's eighty-first birthday, on the twenty-second of August, falls on the fourth Thursday, the day the girls normally get together for a bridge luncheon. Assuming that they have planned a party in her honor, Lavinia has put on the new outfit Dorcas talked her into getting, navy blue crepe with a white collar and matching jacket with three-quarter-length sleeves, even though she never buys new clothes these days. She backs the Lincoln out of the garage, scraping the left rear fender just the teeniest bit, and prepares to drive out to Marge Kramer's on Pill Hill, where all the doctors' widows live.

Lavinia drives slowly because she's been having trouble seeing out of her right eye—it's as though there's a blank spot smack in the center. She plans to arrive just a tad late, to give the others ample chance to get there ahead of her, and decides she might as well take the long way—out Chestnut Street, past Dorcas's new house. Exactly as she's been doing several times a week, when Dorcas isn't there.

For the past four months, ever since Dorcas jumped headlong into this foolish project, Lavinia has been itching to see the inside. She's dropped several hints, but Dorcas keeps putting her off. "It looks pretty awful at this stage," Dorcas says. "Let's wait until I have something nice to show you."

Throughout the summer Dorcas came all the way out from Connecticut twice a month, sometimes three times. "You'll wear yourself out running back and forth," Lavinia told her. "I can keep an eye on Rodney for you, if that would help." But did Dorcas listen? No, she did not. She never does.

Another thing about Dorcas: she's very thin-skinned. Bright as she surely is, she doesn't accept criticism well; even when she was a child, you had to act as though whatever she did was perfect. So far Lavinia has managed to keep her mouth shut about this house, and she has promised herself she will not say *one word* if and when Dorcas gets around to taking her through it.

If and when. She checks her watch, calculates that she has plenty of time, and parks across the street from the house, bumping the curb as she does. She crawls out of the car stiffly and reaches for her cane. Loud music pours from an open window on the second floor. Probably Rodney is working up there. He'll give her a quick tour, of course he will! Lavinia will make it clear to him that Dorcas is not to hear a thing about this little sneak preview. And when Dorcas does decide that the time has come to show her the house, maybe in honor of her birthday, Lavinia will pretend it's a big surprise.

The shutters have been repaired and painted, she observes as she makes her way toward the house, and the old door stripped and refinished and fitted with new brass hardware. She must admit the outside is looking pretty good. But there's a sign in the yard that she's only just noticed:

OPENING SOON
MORGAN HOUSE
Built 1875
AN HISTORIC BED & BREAKFAST

Lavinia doesn't like this *an historic* business. It sounds pretentious. What's wrong with *a historic*? She might mention to Dorcas that this is Pennsylvania, not England, for heaven's sake.

The door is shut, but when Lavinia gingerly turns the knob, it swings open easily. She yoo-hoos, teetering on the threshold, and looks around. Everywhere she looks, she sees devastation. Out of a cloud of dust, Charlie appears. "Hiya, Mrs. B."

"Good morning, Charlie," Lavinia says primly. "Is your uncle here?"

"Went out to Home Depot. Should be back after a bit. Want him to call you?"

Lavinia gazes past Charlie and slowly shakes her head. "No," she says, "I just came by to see how things were going."

There isn't time for the kind of inspection she needs to make here. She should have been dropping by all along, even though Dorcas insisted that she must not and was adamant that she not "interfere" with Rodney.

"Do me a favor, Charlie," she says. "Just don't mention that I was here, all right?"

Charlie grins at her. They've had lots of secrets between them, she and Charlie, so what's one more?

Now she has to hurry in order not to be *too* late. Coey Rothrock's Pontiac, Violet Worley's Cadillac, and Esther

Bowersox's wheezy old Buick are already parked in the circular drive in front of the handsome fieldstone colonial when she pulls in behind them. Grace Metzler, Stella McAllister, and Dorrine Laudenslager would have gotten rides with the others.

Lavinia collects her pocketbook and silver-headed cane and marches up the flagstone walk. Her friends keep telling Marge she ought to give up her house, get a smaller place, what does she want with that big old barn, it's too much for her. But privately they all hope she doesn't sell it because they love coming here. Too late, Lavinia realizes that a fine white plaster dust is clinging to her navy blue pumps, and there's no chance now to wipe them off.

Marge leads the way out to the screened-in porch. "Happy birthday!" her friends holler in their cracking voices, and she throws up her hands in mock surprise.

Despite the heat, they are all dressed to the nines. Marge, the youngest at seventy-seven, has managed to keep her figure and is vain about it. Her yellow linen sheath probably cost a bundle, but she was a doctor's wife and always did spend a lot on clothes.

"Well, how does it feel to be eighty-one?" Coey asks with a sly grin. She's six months younger than Lavinia.

"Funny, I don't feel a day over eighty," Lavinia answers, and everyone chuckles.

Marge says, "Now I have iced tea or lemonade. Which would you like, Lavinia?"

"Gin and tonic," she says, and snickers to show that she's joking. Nobody drinks at noon anymore, which is too damn bad, Lavinia thinks. They claim it makes them sleepy, but so what? They all go home and take naps anyway. "Lemonade would be nice, Marge," she says.

Marge fills her glass from a Waterford pitcher. Then she passes a bowl of nuts, which none of them is supposed to eat because of the salt, and a plate of celery stuffed with cream cheese. On birthdays they break all the rules imposed by their stuffy young doctors.

"How's Dorcas's house coming along?" asks Violet. "Last time I went by there it still looked like a dump."

"Just fine," Lavinia assures her, resenting the criticism and lying through her teeth. "It's going to knock your eyes out when it's done."

What a triumph she enjoyed last spring, reporting to her friends that her daughter was moving back to Juniata to start a business! Let them trump *that*! It was almost as good as the look on their faces at her art show.

"Rod's doing a good job," Lavinia continues. "It was my idea that she hire him, you know." She realizes she's told them this before, and she reaches daintily for another cashew.

"Who?" Stella asks. "Who did she say?"

"Rodney Benner," Grace explains. "That carpenter who fixed up Lavinia's apartment."

"I knew that," Stella says.

"Drive past there again, Vi," Lavinia says. "She's got a sign up. Very handsome. 'Morgan House, A Historic Bed & Breakfast.'" Damned if she'll say *an historic.*

She wants to tell them more, but they've veered suddenly to another topic: Coey's granddaughter is expecting twins. She waits for an opportunity to steer them back, but before she manages to do that, Marge's companion-helper, what's-her-name, the Heckert girl, rings a little brass bell, the signal to move into the dining room.

Marge likes to put on the dog. Years ago, when they first started their bridge lunches, it was deviled ham sandwiches and Campbell's tomato soup and paper napkins. Now on each embroidered place mat at the polished mahogany table Lavinia sees a crystal sherbet dish of something that looks suspiciously like strawberry Jell-o with Cool Whip.

"Jellied madrilene," Marge explains. "With sour cream, and not low-fat, either." She giggles mischievously. "It's like a cold soup."

"Well, I never," remarks Dorrine, poking at hers with a spoon.

"I've had this before," says Esther. "When Herb and I went to New York City."

If I have to listen one more time to her story of New York with Herb, I'll scream, Lavinia thinks. She samples her whatever-it-is. She has never cared for jellied things, aspics and such, but she is too tactful to mention that. "Very pretty," she says. "Festive."

The shrimp salad and popovers that follow are better, and it seems they will be spared Esther's New York story. When the Heckert girl carries in a silver tray of cupcakes with a candle on each, Lavinia's friends sing "Happy Birthday" with discordant gusto. Thank heaven she never had any of them in her choir! Each one blows out her own candle. That's part of the tradition. They're all wishing for another year for themselves.

Esther Bowersox presents the gift, a flat, square box wrapped in sparkly pink paper. Gifts didn't used to be part of the tradition because they all have more things than they know what to do with, but somehow that custom changed along with the menus. Lavinia still has the box of note cards they gave her last year. She's thought of sending them out to Sasha, explaining that they're for thank-you notes and such.

Lavinia opens the box and lifts out a book bound in cloth printed to look like Chinese silk. The pages of the book are blank, thick and ivory-colored.

"It's for your memoirs," Violet explains.

"Read the card," Dorrine orders.

Lavinia pries open the envelope and pulls out a photograph of a naked man with a black rectangle concealing his privates. "Something for your birthday—inside this card is the same photo *without* the black rectangle."

Lavinia is stunned. She glances around. They're all watching her, lips pressing back laughter. She opens the card; it's the same photo, but the black rectangle has been replaced by a hole in the card. Stella guffaws; the rest titter.

Not once since the fiasco of the art exhibit in the spring has a single one of her friends said a word about her paintings. Marge was at the opening; so were Dorrine and Coey. The others have certainly heard about it; they must have gossiped about it behind her back, but to her face they've all pretended that it didn't happen. This is the first hint.

"We figured that out of all of us, you'd probably have the best memoirs," Coey explains.

"The most interesting," Esther adds.

Stella leans toward her. "Write about the naked man," she whispers conspiratorially, and loudly.

Lavinia looks from one to another. "All right," she says. "Maybe I will."

"Include pictures," suggests Dorrine.

In reply Lavinia turns the card around, sticks her little finger through the hole, and waggles it at them. They erupt in shrill, gleeful cackles, and then, as usual, the subject does not so much change as wander off.

❧

The day after her birthday, Lavinia picks up her silver-headed cane and makes a trip up Market Street to Peoples Drugs, where she buys a spiral-bound notebook and three pens—red, blue, and a more expensive black one. Then she crosses the street to the Trolley Stop.

"Having the special today, Mrs. B?" Wanda asks, but Lavinia shakes her head.

"I'll have the rib-eye, please," she says. "Well done." Wanda lifts one of her thin, plucked eyebrows. "I just had another birthday," Lavinia adds coyly. "I've decided to treat myself."

"Well, how about that!" Wanda cries. "You going to tell me how old you are?"

Lavinia shakes her head. "It's a secret." Then she stage-whispers, "Eighty-one," and Wanda pretends to be amazed.

Once Lavinia reached her late seventies, she became by turns secretive and boastful of her age, depending on the audience and the circumstances. She takes pleasure now in looking back over her life, thinking of it as a drama—part tragedy, part comedy, part miracle play—in which she has taken, or was given, the most interesting roles. The birthday present of the handsome blank book has gotten her thinking. The time seems perfect to begin writing about her life. She wishes she'd kept a diary throughout those long decades to jog her memory. Lord knows the material is begging to be used. All she has to do is put her mind to it.

But she can't bring herself to start the first sentence on the first perfect white page. Hence, the cheap notebook. She'll write down whatever comes to mind in the notebook with the blue pen, decide what's best left out and make changes with the red pen and then, when she's satisfied, transfer the finished entry with the elegant black pen into the permanent journal, which will someday be passed on to Dorcas and Sasha as part of their inheritance. The rough version she'll keep for herself, with instructions to destroy it at the time of her death.

Wanda breezes up to the table with a huge platter, the steak hanging off the edge. Silverware and a squirt bottle of ketchup emerge from her apron pockets. "So when's Dorcas moving back for good?"

"Soon. It depends on the house."

"Rod says the place was a real mess. *Challenge*, that's his word. He's in here every day, sometimes twice. He and Marlene are *ffffft*, you know."

"So I've heard." Marlene drones on about the divorce when she does Lavinia's hair, claiming it was all Rod's idea. Lavinia considers telling Wanda about this, but the waitress is headed to her next customers.

Then Rod himself walks in, nods to Lavinia, and straddles a stool at the counter. From the looks of him, he's come straight from Dorcas's challenge. *Folly* might be a better word.

Lavinia saws her way through half the rib-eye, and Wanda brings her a box for the rest. There are times when her refrigerator is taken over by those little white boxes, odds and ends that she forgets about and ends up throwing out.

She leaves the exact amount of the check on the table, plus her customary one-dollar tip, waves to Rod and to Wanda, and heads home with her leftovers and her notebook. Soon, she is lying down on top of the bedspread with an old quilt pulled up to her chin. She closes her eyes, but she's too excited to doze off. She hopes that Dorcas and Sasha will appreciate what she's doing.

It broke her heart that Edgar didn't live to see his granddaughter. He would have been crazy about Sasha, probably spoiled her rotten. And how disappointed he would have been when she ran off and got married to a boy they'd never even met, both just teenagers. At the time Lavinia suspected that Sasha had turned up pregnant, although Dorcas never said so and Lavinia didn't ask. But no baby appeared, and scarcely a year later, Lavinia was informed that Sasha and the boy had parted company. This, Lavinia told Dorcas, was the result of coming from a broken home. She always believed Dorcas was much too lenient with Sasha. "If she'd had some *discipline*," Lavinia said, an obvious truth that infuriated Dorcas.

But that begs the question: If Sasha's upbringing was to blame for her unwise marriage and divorce, what was to blame for Dorcas's?

"The hell with it," Lavinia says aloud, sitting up and feeling for her shoes. She dresses again, makes herself a cup of coffee—the real thing—opens her notebook, and begins.

CHAPTER 11

THE MEMOIRS OF LAVINIA LOUISE MILLER BUCHANAN
I was born on August 22, 1910, the youngest daughter of
Clarence and Edna Yingley Miller, in the town of Juniata, named
for the river on whose banks it stood. [She crosses out "stood"
and substitutes "stands."] *Five older children welcomed me into*
the world: Sarah, called Sister; Clarence Jr., called Clav; Martha;
Kathryn, or Kitty; and Will. Elmer, born between Martha and
Kitty, died as an infant. Clav died in the trenches in France in
1918, the same year Will died of influenza. Martha and Kitty
married and suffered the joys and pangs of life. Sister never mar-
ried. I am the only surviving member of that family.

After three days of writing that makes her fingers ache so
badly she has to take a pain pill, Lavinia begins to wonder if
it wouldn't make sense to buy herself a little tape recorder.
But then someone would have to listen to the tapes and copy
down everything she's said. That could be embarrassing.
She will keep on as she is, painful though that may be.

Lavinia decides not to include much about her brothers
and sisters, except for Sister, ten years older and like a

mother to her after the boys died and Mama stopped taking an interest in anything. Sister made all Lavinia's clothes and did up her hair in the latest style. When Lavinia married Edgar, Sister sewed her wedding dress and a trousseau of delicately embroidered silk. After Lavinia came home from the hospital with the red-faced, squalling Dorcas, Sister stayed with them for three weeks. It was Sister who soothed the colicky infant when Lavinia's breast milk dried up and her nipples cracked and bled, Sister who walked Dorcas through the night so Lavinia could get some sleep.

Once she gets started, memories gush out too fast for Lavinia to write them all down, and not necessarily the ones she wants, or in the order she wants them.

She remembers one muggy summer evening about twenty years ago when Sister arrived unannounced, delivered by City Cab. Lavinia had just gotten home from the office, hot and tired and not entirely pleased to have drop-in company, even Sister.

After excusing herself to yank off her girdle and nylons, Lavinia mixed up a pitcher of lemonade and spiked her own glass with a shot of gin, something she'd learned from Edgar. She put the two glasses and a plate of Ritz crackers and a jar of pimiento cheese on a tray and carried them out to the porch.

Watching Sister spread cheese on a cracker, Lavinia realized with a shock how much Sister had aged, how slow and painful her movements had become. "How've you been feeling?" Lavinia asked, suddenly worried.

"Well, that's just it. Not so good. I've had my name on the list out at Sylvan Manor, and they called last week that there's an opening."

"You should have talked this over with me!" Lavinia cried. "There must be some other way!"

Even as she said it, Lavinia knew that the "other way" might involve moving Sister in with her. It's what she should have done, she admits that now; there she was with that big empty house, and gone most of the day anyhow.

Sister smiled and shook her head, as though she'd read Lavinia's mind. "It wouldn't work, us living together. You know that as well as I do." She sipped her lemonade. "There's some things I need to get off my chest. I'm the one who told Pop about Nicholas."

Lavinia jolted back in her chair. "Told him *what?*"

"That you were meeting him out at the stoneyard that summer. Nicholas."

Lavinia laid her hand on her chest and drew a slow breath, trying to calm herself. "How did you know?"

"I followed you. I saw you with him. More than once."

Lavinia stared at her. "You waited all these years to tell me this? Why are you telling me now?"

Sister smiled sadly. "To clear my guilty conscience. This is one of the matters I want to settle."

Lavinia drained her glass. She'd felt woozy. "Why did you tell Pop?"

"I believed it was my responsibility. Also," Sister added, "and don't you dare laugh at this, but I think I was a little bit in love with Nicholas myself."

"You were jealous."

"All right."

"You were older than him."

"Not by much. A couple of years."

"I'll be right back," Lavinia said, heading for the kitchen.

"Bring the gin bottle with you, Lovey," Sister called after her. "I could use a shot of that myself."

❧❦❧

Nicholas Santangelo. How long has it been? On the last page of the notebook, she does a quick calculation: sixty-five years! Six and a half decades, and her memories of him are clearer than yesterday's. She's forgotten nothing.

She had been so crazy for him that her yearning was like a ringing in her ears, flashes of light behind her eyelids. She thought she'd die when she found out he was gone.

It was 1927 and she was not quite seventeen.

As soon as school was out, Pop had moved Mama and Sister and Lavinia out to the farm for the summer, thinking it would do Mama good. Sister and Lavinia still shared a room, even though Martha and Kitty were both married by then and their old room was empty. But the girls were used to being together, sleeping in the same bed.

On a night in the middle of June, when the moon was full and the cicadas were singing their loudest, Lavinia waited until Sister was asleep, and then she crept out of their bed and hurried out to the barn. She swapped her thin nightdress for an old pair of overalls and a man's shirt she'd hidden behind some bales of hay, along with the bicycle (it had belonged to Will, but after his death she found it and taught herself to ride, keeping out of Mama's sight). She wheeled the bike silently through the apple orchard until she reached the road; then she pedaled furiously to the stoneyard. Nicholas was waiting for her there.

They had become acquainted when she'd gone several times to the stoneyard with her father. She liked to watch the carvers chipping at the huge slabs of granite and marble. The youngest and handsomest of the men had smiled at her. She asked his name; Nicholas, he said. He was tall and broad-shouldered, with curly black hair, eyes dark and rich as molasses, and a brilliant smile, although when he laughed she saw that a tooth was missing on each side. He had hard, muscular arms and large, rough hands. She knew better than to start a conversation when anyone was watching. "We can talk more if I come here tonight," she'd whispered boldly.

Lavinia marvels now at her youthful insouciance. *What did I think I was doing?*

That night Nicholas guided her through the stoneyard and showed her graceful urns with flaring handles, kneeling angels with each fold of draped cloth, each feather on the arched wings precisely carved, bouquets of lilies and praying hands and the head of Christ with a crown of thorns incised in low relief.

Cutting names and dates and simple ornamentation into the tombstones, the job for which he'd been hired, was easy for him, he told her. His uncles, trained in Italy, had taught him how to carve the large figures. Someday, he said, he would be a sculptor. A fine artist.

"You're already a fine artist," she said, as though she were capable of judging.

His callused hands were surprisingly tender when they touched her face. He told her she was beautiful—*bella*—and that she would be in his sculpture.

By the time of the new moon, she was pedaling out to the stoneyard nearly every night.

Someday, she thought, after Nicholas had proven himself to her father, shown that he was a carver capable of true artistic accomplishment, and after he had been able to save up enough money, they would elope. There would be no more furtive meetings, although part of the thrill was the secrecy. Here was one part of her life that even Sister knew nothing about.

After many passionate kisses behind a stand of bushes some distance from the shack where he stayed with his uncles, Nicholas persuaded her to roll up her overalls, so that he could study the delicate modeling of her knees and calves; it was easier to remove them. Next, she unbuttoned her shirt and let him lift it over her head. Bit by bit, she took everything off, including her underthings, while Nicholas gazed at her reverently. Finally she stood before him completely naked.

"Beautiful," Nicholas said again and again. She thought she saw tears in his eyes. *"Bella. Bellissima."*

The night air turned cool, and Lavinia reached for her clothes, strewn around on the damp grass. "Now you," she said.

He looked at her as though he didn't understand.

"Your turn to take your clothes off." She stepped back into her underthings. "Turnabout is fair play."

Shyly, he turned his back and shucked off his trousers. Now fully clothed herself, Lavinia sat on the ground, one bare ankle crossed over the other, and watched him as reverently as he had gazed at her. *Magnificent!* she thought, studying his strong back and solid buttocks. "Now turn around, please."

The only male she'd seen naked was her brother, Will, when they had bathed him, trying to bring down his fever, and that had not prepared her for the sight of Nicholas's penis. She gasped and stared. He moved closer. "Touch," he whispered. "Please."

Timidly, she reached out and with the tips of her fingers stroked the limp pink thing, nestled in its bed of wiry hair. Magically, it enlarged, stiffened, sprang up at her. She snatched away her hand. He begged her, calling her *cara mia,* and she obeyed, too fascinated to protest. He clamped his fist over her fingers and groaned, a low growl that frightened her, and as she tried to scramble away from him, he grabbed her and held her tight against him.

Then he was full of apologies. He had made a mess on her overalls. She was glad she wasn't wearing one of her good dresses.

"Good Lord," Lavinia mutters now, reading over her scribbled notes. The phone rings, but she ignores it, scarcely hears it. She is reliving that summer, intent upon every moment.

Later, she remembers, she rode back to the farm, hid the bike and the overalls, which she had to find a way to wash, and crept into the house. She slid between the cool linen sheets beside Sister, still sleeping soundly.

After that first evening, Nicholas often brought a pad and pencil, and, while they talked, before he asked her to touch his penis—they had a pet name for it now, "Brother Giovanni"—he sketched her body with long, sinuous lines. "Tell me stories," she begged, "about when you were a child."

He indulged her. He had been born in Carrara, he said, and came to America with his father and uncles when he was a boy. He described the village where he was born, the stone house where his grandparents still lived, the wine his grandfather made, his grandmother's soups and bread. Someday, he said, he would go back to visit. He taught her a few phrases in Italian, explaining that she would need them when she went with him. He smiled his charming grin. She was enraptured.

Other times he talked of his plans to move to Philadelphia, where he had cousins. A good place for an artist, he said.

She had no stories for Nicholas. Her life had only begun that summer. Before, she had been just a pampered child.

The only thing she knew for sure at that moment was how much she loved him. Their kisses had become deeply passionate, and when he said, "Brother Giovanni is lonely. He wants you to hold him," she did so gladly.

Touch me, Nicholas. Had she actually said that? What was she doing? His rough stone-carver's hands, now so gentle, began to caress her breasts, circled the soft swelling of her navel, explored her curly blond thatch, and then slid between her legs into a dampness that embarrassed her. Her mind warned her to stop him, but her body ignored the warning and urged him to go on. Helpless against the rush of desire, she pressed her face against his chest and wept. He guided her hand once more to Giovanni.

Early in August, Nicholas had finished another drawing and, as they lay in the deep grass, she told him that in a few weeks her father would move her back into town for the start of school—she would be a senior. How would she ever manage to see Nicholas again?

In reply, Nicholas began his familiar kissing and stroking that led to such pleasure. But this time, as her thighs opened to his hand, she felt Brother Giovanni pressing insistently between her legs. A thought, loosely formed, swam through her brain: *This is dangerous, what if—?*

In no way was she prepared for this. But as she rose to meet him, her thoughts broke apart—*Oh, God!*—the pieces scattered by her love for him, her need to show him that love.

Afterward, though, frightened by the blood and the unexpected pain and his apologies—he had not intended to hurt her, he begged her forgiveness—the thought took on a definite shape: *This is how it happens, isn't it? Babies conceived?* She wasn't certain. No one had spoken to her about such matters. She was too young to be concerned, Sister had told her. But Nicholas assured her that she had nothing to worry about, he had withdrawn in time. There was the proof, spread stickily across her belly.

She believed she could trust him, and the next time he took her, naked, into his arms, she pushed aside any remaining fears. She wanted their bodies joined as she told herself their hearts were. If "it" happened, she decided, she and Nicholas would simply marry right away. They would adore and keep to each other forever, and her wrathful father would simply have to live with that.

She existed for their hours together, always tingling with desire but fearful of discovery. One morning, as she and Sister were eating breakfast, Sister reached over and pulled a wisp of grass from her hair.

Nicholas was a patient teacher, and Lavinia a devoted pupil. The pain disappeared, the pleasure increased. Lavinia looked pityingly at Sister, who had never experienced such love.

On the night of her seventeenth birthday, August 22, she rode to the stoneyard, later than usual—there had been a little celebration with ice cream and cake. Nicholas wasn't there. She waited and waited; in tears, she rode home alone. It was the same the next night, and the next. Nicholas had disappeared, had left her without a word or a sign. "By the way, I'm looking for a new stonecutter. Young Santangelo is gone," Pop announced in a hard, angry voice at Sunday dinner, after they'd come home from church.

Lavinia stared at the roast chicken on her plate. "Gone?" she whispered.

"Family emergency, I believe."

Lavinia struggled to hide her grief, too numbed with pain even to realize her good fortune when her menses came a few days later. Then school began, and she once again had a number of boys vying for her attention. It was easy to ignore them. Mama's health worsened until she was scarcely able to get out of bed. When she died quietly soon after New Year's, a heavy cloud settled over the household.

She never told anyone about Nicholas, not even her best friend. And certainly not Sister. But she has never forgotten him. Memories of Nicholas had a way of coming to her at the oddest times through the years—a visit to Rocco's Ristorante could trigger a whole slew of them.

Sometimes Lavinia cannot remember the simplest thing—the name of her doctor, for example, or her own zip code—but she has not forgotten Nicholas's body, or the color of his eyes. Only in the past few years has she allowed herself to paint him—over and over, recalling every angle and curve, every bone and sinew, the slightly oily feel of the skin on his muscular back, the coarse texture of his hair as she buried her fingers in it so long ago. And then she began to paint herself, too, the way Nicholas must have seen her, the way they would have been.

❧

It takes Lavinia days to write the story of Nicholas. She isn't sure how much of this to transfer to the book she plans to leave to Dorcas and Sasha. How honest should you be in your memoirs? Already Nicholas has created a scandal. All that furor when she hung those paintings for the art show! What will it be like when she reveals in her memoirs the story behind the paintings?

Then she thinks: *Why worry? I'll be dead when they read it!*

CHAPTER 12

"An open house the end of October? That's not even six weeks from now!" Lavinia is incredulous. "Dorcas, listen to me, you're just asking for more headaches. Begging for them!"

Dorcas has finally broken down and taken Lavinia on a tour of the house. But after such a long wait to see the interior, Lavinia is not impressed. Anything *but*. It's true that the place looks pretty good now from the outside, but just look at this kitchen! New plumbing has been roughed in, but the cabinetry isn't ready or the appliances hooked up or the floors sanded. The sheetrocking is finished and the woodwork stripped, but there's not a lick of fresh paint anywhere, just color chips tacked to the walls of each room.

"What a mess," Lavinia says grimly, laboring up the stairs to the bedrooms.

"It'll get done, Mother," Dorcas insists. "Don't worry."

"*I'm* not the one who's worrying. And if *you're* not worried, you certainly should be."

Lavinia hears Dorcas's long-suffering sigh. "Just look at these colors," Dorcas says with false-sounding cheeriness. "Cloudberry Blue, Buttercream Yellow, Smoky Rose. Aren't they beautiful? Each room will have a different color scheme, see, and a different name. I'm still thinking about the names."

Lavinia glances at the color chips, which strike her as much too bright—almost gaudy. She wishes she could be more enthusiastic—*supportive* is the word they use now—but she can't. "Just *who* do you think is going to stay here during the winter?" Lavinia wants to know. "Makes more sense to take your time, work on things slowly, and open next spring."

But Dorcas doesn't want to hear it. "There will still be plenty of odds and ends to finish up over the winter," she insists stubbornly. "The third floor, for instance. I'm thinking of having Rod finish the two small bedrooms up there."

"How do you know you'll even need those extra rooms? A waste of money if you don't." She's unable to resist adding, "But maybe you don't have to worry about money like the rest of us."

Dorcas has set up camp in one of the second-floor bedrooms—"This was Jimmy O'Brien's old room"—with a cot and an ice chest and a microwave that Rootie loaned her until the refrigerator and stove are connected. Now she insists on staying alone here at night, a decision that resulted in an argument a week or so ago. Dorcas had been complaining that Lavinia's sofa bed bothered her back, and she'd gotten snappish at even the simplest questions, the most reasonable requests for information. "I'm not a child," she said. "I should not have to account for where I'm going every time I go out the door and when I'll be back." Then she announced that she'd decided to move into Morgan House just as it was.

Lavinia registered her disapproval. "Why would you want to live like a vagabond when you've got a comfortable place?"

"I can get up in the middle of the night and roam around and think about how I want each room," Dorcas said. "There are dozens of little decisions that have to be made, and it's easier if I can be alone there to *ponder.*"

"This is still a very small town, you know, and people do talk," Lavinia pointed out. "They'll wonder why you want to sleep in that empty old house. It's common knowledge that Rodney Benner's over there at all hours. I'd ponder *that*, if I were you." Then she added, "But then nobody can ever tell you anything. You've always done exactly as you please, so I suppose nothing *I* say will make the slightest bit of difference."

Lavinia had nearly forgotten how stubborn and intractable and plain pig-headed Dorcas could be.

They start down the stairs, moving slowly. The tour is over. When they reach the front hall, Dorcas starts nudging her toward the front door. "Want a ride home?" Dorcas asks.

"No need to drive me. I can walk from here." Dorcas does not, Lavinia notices, offer to walk with her.

It's not until Lavinia is crossing Five Points that Dorcas's remark hits home: *This was Jimmy O'Brien's old room.* Now how would Dorcas know that, unless she'd been up there with him? Lavinia wonders what all was actually going on between those two. Surely nothing, him going into the priesthood and all, but *still*!

Passing the Emporium, with a display of fall outfits that look tackier than ever, Lavinia remembers the day Dorcas rushed home from school with the exciting news that Jimmy had invited her to the sophomore hop. "I need a dress," she said. According to Dorcas, Rootie and Marlene had already bought dresses at the Emporium—Marlene's was pink taffeta and Rootie's had a sweetheart neckline—but Lavinia put her foot down and insisted that they go to Wasserman's Ladies Shop, where Lavinia shopped for her own clothes.

"Something simple and smart," Lavinia instructed Coey Rothrock, who'd worked at Wasserman's for years, since her husband had his stroke. "Nothing frilly." She looked pointedly at Dorcas, who glared back. Her daughter's taste was nothing like Lavinia's; Dorcas *liked* frilly. *Loved* it, in fact.

"I have just the thing," Coey said. "It will be perfect on you, Dorcas, wait and see." The dress she brought out was dark green faille with a Peter Pan collar and a cummerbund sash—the newest thing, according to Coey—and green and red plaid ruffles that cascaded down the back from waist to hem.

"Remember, dear, when you're dancing with a boy, everybody sees you from the rear, not the front, so you have the sash tied like so, with the ends hanging down over the ruffles for back interest, and you look, well, just *super*, that's all I can say, because you can see for yourself. And I'll tell you what"—Coey pinched the loose fabric in the top—"let's just sneak a couple of falsies in the front here, to give you a little more bosom. There! Now isn't that just darling? Mother, what do you think?"

Maybe not darling, Lavinia thought, but not bad. "Looks very nice on you, Dorcas," Lavinia said, careful not to react too enthusiastically.

Dorcas twirled in front of the full-length mirror and gawked over her shoulder at the rear view. Her lip was trembling. "Don't you have it in *blue*? I *hate* green," she complained. "It makes me look bilious—Rootie and Marlene said so." She clamped her arms across her padded chest and sulked.

Lavinia and Coey exchanged glances. "But this number doesn't come in blue," Coey said in a reasonable tone. "Hunter is all the rage this year. You're really in style with this color. Very up-to-date without being, you know, *faddish*. Everyone's a little tired of blue, see. But of course if you don't like it, honey, why that's your decision."

There was a long silence, during which Lavinia managed, barely, to keep her mouth shut. "Okay," Dorcas muttered at last. "Just to satisfy *you*." She shot her mother a hateful look.

"Don't do me any favors!" Lavinia snapped. "Have you even looked at the price tag on this dress? Your father will have a fit." Which was untrue, because they both knew Edgar would have bought Dorcas the moon if she'd asked for it.

That night after they'd finished supper and Dorcas was piling dirty dishes into the dishpan, Edgar poked his head into the kitchen. "Time for the dress rehearsal," he said. "Put on your ball gown and slippers, Cinderella, so you can get used to dancing in them."

Lavinia could have cheerfully dumped the whole pan of dirty dishwater over Edgar's balding head. The man had no consideration. "Go," she said, angrily flapping the dishrag at Dorcas. "The dishes will still be here."

Twenty minutes later, enough time for Lavinia, tight-lipped, to finish the damned dishes herself, just to get them out of the way, Dorcas descended the stairs in the new green dress and the new black suede shoes with ankle straps. Edgar was putting a record on the turntable. His eyes lit up when he saw her. "May I have the pleasure of this dance?" he asked.

Lavinia stood in the doorway, gripping a soggy dish towel, as Edgar demonstrated: ONE-two-three ONE-two-three, snapping his fingers crisply on the downbeat. He showed Dorcas how to mirror his simple box step, his hands on her waist, her hands resting trustingly on his shoulders. "Here we go!" he said, and waltzed Dorcas across the living room, swooping through the dining room and back while she giggled and stumbled clumsily along with him.

"Lavinia, run and get the camera and take a picture!" Edgar called out. Dorcas flashed her mother a triumphant smile. The picture is pasted in one of the old albums.

Every evening for the next three weeks, except on Tuesdays when Edgar had a Lions Club meeting, there was another lesson. While Lavinia watched, fuming silently, they progressed from the waltz to the two-step and some basic swing, although she doubted if any youngsters still danced this way. Dorcas probably knew that and was leading Edgar on. Here was her daughter, a girl who simply *could not* hang up her clothes but dropped everything on the floor of her room as though she had a maid following her around. A girl who *could not* remember that she was supposed to dry and put away the dishes every night, whether or not her father decided to give her a dancing lesson. A girl whose endless, silly conversations with Rootie tied up the phone for an hour at a time even though Lavinia had told her *repeatedly* that calls had to be kept to no more than fifteen minutes.

"Someday, Dorcas," Lavinia used to say through gritted teeth, "when you have a daughter of your own, you'll find out what it's *like*."

Lavinia now has a pretty good idea that Sasha gave Dorcas a run for her money, even more than Dorcas gave *her*.

But Dorcas obviously caved in too easily and just let Sasha run wild. Otherwise, Sasha would have learned to write thank-you notes when they were due.

Lavinia arrives at her house and rides the electric seat up to her apartment. Just as soon as she's had a chance to rest her eyes, she must get out to her studio. She has begun a painting of Morgan House as a surprise for Dorcas, and she wants to finish it in time for the opening. She had Charlie take some pictures of the house, and she's using them as a guide. It's not to be a painting of the house as it looks today but the way she remembers it when she was seventeen and walked by it every day on her way to school.

"You're not near ready," Lavinia says three weeks before the open house is scheduled. "You've still got acres of walls to paint. I'd help you if I could, Dorcas, but I'm just not able."

"I don't need your help with the painting, Mother," Dorcas growls in a voice that could bend steel. "I just need names of people who should get invitations. When the Art League has an exhibit, don't you have a list of people you send announcements to?"

Lavinia sniffs. "No, but I'll see what I can find for you."

Over the next two days, during the time she'd normally be working on her memoirs, she sits at her desk and combs through her address book. This gets her down, though, because so many names have been crossed out, marked with a D and a date, if she knows it. A lot of the survivors in the book are out-of-towners, but there is still a fair number of locals.

On a pleasant Sunday afternoon, Lavinia takes her list over to Dorcas. Rootie is there, too, addressing envelopes.

It's like watching the two of them when they were in high school, working on the yearbook together, just the goofiest pair. In some ways they seem not to have improved much, still laughing over nothing.

While the girls work, Lavinia prowls around to see what, if any, progress has been made. She discovers that Dorcas has set up a workshop in the parlor. She and Rootie have been scouring secondhand stores around the county in search of old furniture—scarred chests of drawers and odd tables and rocking chairs with chunks of veneer missing. Nothing but junk, in Lavinia's opinion, that they're "rehabilitating."

"That cheap oak is worthless," Lavinia warns them. "A waste of time and trouble, to say nothing of money. Beats me, why you'd want to bother with it."

"It's all still serviceable, Mrs. B," Rootie says, not even looking up. "Once we get them fixed up and painted, put some new knobs on them and such, they'll look just fine."

"What about that pair of saltware crocks?" Lavinia demands. "Both of them are cracked."

"Don't know yet," Dorcas murmurs.

"And you have all that good stuff of Stella's," she says, refusing to give up. Dorcas doesn't reply.

Several days later, Lavinia's invitation arrives in the mail. She just hopes this open house does not turn out to be a disaster.

CHAPTER 13

Morgan House, An Historic Bed & Breakfast, opens its doors to the public during an early winter storm that dumps fourteen inches of wet snow on Juniata and brings the town to a standstill.

The storm blows in late Saturday afternoon while Dorcas is in State College, doing last-minute grocery shopping for things she claims she can't find in Juniata. "Like what?" Lavinia asks curiously.

"Phyllo leaves," Dorcas replies, "for the baked brie."

"Nobody knows what that is, Dorcas."

"Then they'll find out."

Lavinia calls every half hour, hanging up when the answering machine comes on, until Dorcas gets back safely. "Well, I hope those leaves were worth worrying everybody to death," she says.

Before she goes to bed, Lavinia remembers that this is the weekend to turn the clocks back. She wonders if Dorcas thought of that. Even though she knows Dorcas is busy getting ready and probably doesn't want to be bothered, she decides that this qualifies as a near-emergency. She dials Dorcas's number, but the machine picks up again: "Hello! You've reached Morgan House," says Dorcas's recorded voice. "No one can come to the phone right now, but your call is important to us."

What baloney! Lavinia hates these things, but she clears her throat and, when the recording stops, says, "Just a reminder to change your clocks, Dorcas. Fall back!"

Lavinia is up and down all night, watching the snow accumulate. Sunday morning she calls again, in case Dorcas hasn't listened to her messages yet. "Fall back, Dorcas, fall back!"

"I remembered, Mother. But thank you."

Lavinia can tell when Dorcas doesn't want to talk. She considers offering to come over early to help set up but thinks better of it. Dorcas has made it plain that she doesn't want her help.

Next, Lavinia calls Charlie to remind him that he's to pick her up at a quarter of two and also to make sure he remembered to fall back. There's no answer. Maybe they've gone to church. Then she hears scraping beneath her window; it's Charlie, shoveling her sidewalk.

At noon Lavinia heats a little soup and at one o'clock, after she's rested her eyes for a few minutes, she puts on her lavender suit and the amethyst pin Edgar gave her on their last anniversary. At one-thirty Charlie is back, dressed up in a jacket and tie but still wearing those awful sneakers, and warms up her car. At a quarter of two, Lavinia drapes over her shoulders the mink coat she bought herself as a retirement present, and pulls on plastic rain booties and a pleated rain bonnet.

Now, at five minutes of two, Lavinia's old Lincoln, piloted by Charlie, docks in front of Morgan House. Snow is still coming down, and Charlie helps Lavinia negotiate the slushy sidewalk. The saltware crocks are by the front door, filled with greens.

"Awful weather!" she announces, shucking off the booties and bonnet and handing Dorcas her coat. "Gave me an excuse to skip church this morning. I hope somebody shows up this afternoon." She takes a hard look at Dorcas. "Good Lord, what have you done to your *hair?*

"It's just a rinse," Dorcas says, ducking her head, as though she expects Lavinia's disapproval. "Marlene talked me into it."

Lavinia scrutinizes her from all sides. "Looks kind of oddball to me." She resists saying that it looks kind of *cheap.* Then she takes in Dorcas's outfit, black pants and a white blouse, something a waiter might wear. "Aren't you going to change clothes?"

"I already did. This is what I'm wearing this afternoon."

"I thought you'd get dressed up, that's all."

"I *am* dressed up."

"Pants! That's not being dressed up."

"For me, this is dressed up, Mother. Now why don't you come and take a look at the table?"

Lavinia stares. She never would have picked that deep rose that Dorcas has painted the walls, but the color does set off Stella McAllister's antiques very nicely. A fire crackles in the fireplace, and her painting of Morgan House hangs above it. In the middle of the table is a bouquet of white roses in a crystal bowl.

"Well, it does look pretty," Lavinia admits. "Who sent the roses?"

"Barbara Lambert, my old neighbor. Remember Barbara?"

"The one with the awful laugh? Like a rusty gate?"

Lavinia circles the table. Platters of cold appetizers are attractively arranged and trivets set out for the hot dishes. She doesn't recognize half the food. She pauses by something that resembles a meatloaf with brightly colored stripes. "What is *that?*"

"Vegetable paté," Dorcas says. "Try some on a cracker."

"No, *thank you*," says Lavinia firmly. "But a cup of coffee would hit the spot, if you don't mind. And I'll have one of those cookies."

Lavinia plants herself at a small table by the window and opens the leather-bound guest book she brought as a gift for Dorcas. From where she sits she can catch people coming and going and get them to sign it, and she can also admire her painting of Morgan House. She's pleased with the way it came out—for one thing, there's no dumb "An Historic Bed & Breakfast" sign. Instead, there's the figure of a young girl walking by with an armful of schoolbooks, and a man with a rake stands in the yard. It could be the owner, but of course it's not—it's Nicholas, and the girl is herself. Her secret.

Rootie pokes her head in from the kitchen to say hello. "I've been here since eight," she says. "I forgot to fall back." Lavinia has her sign the guest book, the first official visitor to Morgan House.

"These cookies are stale," Lavinia complains to Dorcas. "I can hardly bite into them. I'm afraid I might break a tooth."

"They're biscotti, Mother. They're Italian. And hard. You're supposed to dunk them in coffee."

The doorbell rings. "Here we go!" says Dorcas and hurries to open the door. It's Marlene, dressed to kill in a black and purple satin outfit with sequins and a dangerously plunging neckline. The dress fits like paint. "Dorcas!" Marlene cries. "You look fabulous! Don't you love the hair? It makes you look years younger!"

Lavinia snorts.

Over the next three hours, dozens of guests track icy clumps of melting snow over the polished floors and (fake) Oriental carpets. They help themselves to mulled wine from an ironstone tureen and cautiously sample the food. Only the bravest try the vegetable paté. Rootie trots back and forth from the kitchen, keeping the tureen filled and the platters replenished. Something called baked brie, puffy and golden from the oven, elicits appreciative murmurs.

"It's made with phyllo leaves," Lavinia explains from her perch. "I never heard of it either. Now that over there, with the orange and green stripes, that's *vegetable paté.* Try it on a *water biscuit,*" she says encouragingly. "And those cookies are *biscotti,* which Italians dunk in their coffee, or so I'm told." *I'll bet Nicholas never ate anything like this in his life.*

Rod has let himself in through the backdoor, and Lavinia watches how he manages to keep at least one room between himself and Marlene. Marlene, meanwhile, angles so that Rod will get an eyeful of her every time he turns around. He seems relieved to take Don Stamm and a couple of other men down to the cellar, presumably to look at the furnace—old, but still functioning.

She watches as Debbie Larber, her attorney's wife, holds one of Stella's china plates up to the light, squinting to see if it's porcelain.

Sharon Dieter, the real estate saleswoman, whom Lavinia has never liked—she's too brassy—leads tours to the upstairs bedrooms, explaining the history of the house. "It was built in 1870 by William Alfred Morgan. At that time it was one of our finest residences, and thanks to Dorcas, it is again." She'll be showing them the William &

Anna Suite with its cozy fireplace, the Lilac Room and the Daisy Room, which do look sunny even on a gray and wintry day like this one, and Jimmy's room, now called the Lily of the Valley Room.

When Stella McAllister arrives with Coey and Grace, she stares at her old table and chairs in the dining room and bursts into tears. Lavinia pats Stella's arm and says soothingly, "Look what a beautiful home your things have here."

"A class act, Dorcas," pronounces Dr. Wilson, a tall, wattled man with a stiff brush of silvery hair. His wife, called Brownie, an Alabaman whose syrupy vowels have survived intact nearly thirty years in central Pennsylvania, agrees.

"Honey, it's a fine place to send doctors visiting the hospital for a medical conference, or anyone who plain just wants to get away from it all."

Lavinia hopes she's right.

Harriet Stamm, a thin, parched woman, pecks Lavinia on the cheek and then sidles over to inspect the Morgan House painting. She practically gets her nose up against the two figures—probably, Lavinia thinks, to make sure they have clothes on.

Lavinia recalls now that a dealer in Harrisburg contacted her recently to buy one of her nude paintings for a client. She told him they weren't for sale. He asked if she'd paint another one, and Lavinia said she'd think about it. He didn't say who his client was. She has her suspicions, though: the Stamms.

Lots of other people show up as well, including a few she doesn't recognize, and she thought she knew everybody. Every one of her bridge-playing friends come by, and even Reverend Burkholder puts in an appearance, dressed in his dusty black suit and a white clerical collar. The backward collar is something new and not entirely approved of by the congregation. Lavinia personally thinks it's entirely too popish.

The afternoon passes, and the guests—the Wilsons, the Larbers, the Stamms, the same people who patronize Art League openings and sit on the board of the historical society—squeeze Lavinia's hand and tell her how glad they are that Dorcas has come back to Juniata and what a good thing she's done to bring the lovely old house back to life. They tuck Morgan House brochures into their purses and promise that the next time they have an overflow of houseguests, they'll be sure to send them over. They wish Dorcas all the luck in the world.

It's after five o'clock when the last guests finally leave. Lavinia, worn out, steps into the kitchen, hunting for Charlie to take her home, and finds Dorcas and Rootie collapsed at the kitchen table. "Charlie's down in the basement with Rod," Dorcas says, "checking on the furnace. It's making funny noises."

Rootie pulls out a chair for her. "Sit down, Mrs. B," she says, and Lavinia sits.

"So what do you think?" Dorcas asks.

"I think you should go straight to bed and get some rest," Lavinia advises. Dorcas ignores her words.

"A smashing success," Rootie says. "They loved it. It was brilliant."

"I feel so good about it that I just told Rod to go ahead and finish the two small bedrooms on the third floor," Dorcas announces and ladles herself a cup of mulled wine.

Lavinia pulls a long face to show her disapproval. Dorcas pretends not to notice.

"You'll definitely need the space," Rootie continues enthusiastically. "Everybody who was anybody was here. Even my asshole boss came. Dirty Dave Dixon."

Lavinia flinches at the word "asshole."

"I can't place him," Dorcas says. "What does he look like?"

"A weasel. Pointy features. Twitchy little mustache. You didn't miss anything. Shirley Varner was here, too. Did you get a chance to talk to her? She's a good person to know. Biggest heart in the world. Too bad, all the talk about her."

"Why? What's she done?"

"Everybody thinks she's gay. She wears her hair short, and one patron insists she can tell by Shirley's walk. There have been parents in the library who don't want her doing Story Book Time with their kids, because she might corrupt the little buggers. Listen, is there any more of that mulled wine?"

Oh, for God's sake! Lavinia pushes herself to her feet. "I've got to get home," she says. "Time for my pills."

Dorcas and Rootie both look up at her, startled, as though they've forgotten she's there. Just then Charlie and Rod tramp up the cellar stairs.

Lavinia assembles her mink coat, the plastic booties, her purse, her gloves, her silver-headed cane. Charlie has gone out to warm up the car. She pokes her head in the kitchen to say good-bye.

Rootie is leaning close to Rod, urging him to try the last of the vegetable paté. "Go ahead," she urges. "Live dangerously."

Lavinia recognizes the lilt in Rootie's voice. *Tsk tsk!* she thinks. "Good-bye, all," she says.

"Take care, Mrs. B!" Rootie turns and winks.

Dorcas throws on a shawl and walks with her out to the car. Lavinia pats Dorcas on the arm. "It was wonderful, Dorcas," she says. "Just splendid. Everybody thought so." But she can't resist adding, "Now you just have to convince some paying guests," and heads off into the gathering darkness.

CHAPTER 14

On Christmas Eve, at exactly five o'clock according to the radio, Dorcas and Lavinia light a bayberry candle. "It brings good luck if it burns all the way down," Lavinia reminds her daughter, instantly remembering that she says this every Christmas.

"You used to worry that it would burn the house down while we were at church. Daddy talked you into leaving it in the sink."

"Bathtub," Lavinia says. "I leave it in the bathtub."

Lavinia has fixed a casserole she calls "schnitzel," the mixture of ground beef, noodles, and canned tomatoes she has always served on Christmas Eve, accompanied by a slice of canned pineapple centered on a lettuce leaf with a maraschino cherry in the hole of the pineapple, in honor of the holiday. She served this meal the first time Alex came to visit at Christmas, and it turned out he thought schnitzel meant veal cutlets. She can still picture his expression as he was presented with her specialty.

"How is the work progressing on the attic rooms?" Lavinia asks, spooning some of the casserole onto her plate.

"They're finished. Rod and Charlie moved the furniture up there a couple of days ago. The old spindle bed and the butterfly quilt that Sister made look great."

Lavinia dabs her lips with a linen napkin. "Now all you need is some customers."

The bayberry candle is still flickering in the bathtub when they return from the Christmas Eve service. Dorcas uses the phone in the bedroom to call Sasha—it would be a little past six in California—and Lavinia picks up the extension in the kitchen.

After a half dozen rings, Sasha answers. "Merry Christmas, Mom." She sounds garbled, as though her mouth is full. "Got your check. Thanks. You shouldn't have sent anything this year. I even said that, didn't I? If I didn't, I meant to. Because you must be even shorter on cash than I am."

"Let's hope it's only temporary," Dorcas says. "Thanks for the tape. I haven't listened to it yet, but it looks like it should be interesting." *What tape is that?* Lavinia wonders.

"I hope you like it. Crime and Punishment is a feminist band. The musicians are friends of mine."

"Sharing your appreciation of Dostoyevsky."

"Who?"

"A Russian writer. He wrote a book called *Crime and Punishment.* I thought it had something to do with that."

Lavinia listens impatiently as her daughter and granddaughter grope for things to talk about. Sasha asks how the B&B is going; Dorcas says fine but slow so far and tells her about the friends of Brownie Wilson who came from Alabama for four days and complained about everything from low water pressure to cats yowling outside their window. Then Dorcas asks how the film script is going, and Sasha says okay.

Lavinia clears her throat.

"Lovey, is that you?" Sasha asks.

While Lavinia is talking, among the pleasantries remind-ing Sasha of the virtues of thank-you notes, she watches her daughter wander around the small living room. Dorcas lifts the large poinsettia on the coffee table and picks up the card tucked under it. Lavinia knows what it says: "Seasons Greetings from Alex and Ellen." Dorcas glances at it, frowns, and slips it back under the plant. Next she shuffles through the Christmas cards piled on a silver tray, glancing at the sig-natures. As Lavinia finishes her final admonition and wishes Sasha a Merry Christmas, Dorcas comes upon a card with a snapshot enclosed. Dorcas waves the picture triumphantly as Lavinia hangs up the phone.

An elderly woman, gaunt and frail, sits stiffly in a wing chair, staring at the camera. On her lap is a baby, grinning and toothless. A slim, pretty, young woman crouches next to the chair and reaches a protective hand toward the baby. Behind her a bulky woman in a pink pants suit and glasses with large pink frames smiles broadly beneath a pile of metallic blond curls. The elderly woman is Lavinia's oldest friend, Frannie Yoder. The bulky woman in pink is Frannie's daughter, Becca, once possessed of beauty, glamour, sophistication—all those things that poor Dorcas yearned for and did not have during those awful, awkward adolescent years that Lavinia thought would never end.

Lavinia peers over Dorcas's shoulder at the snapshot. "Becca put on a little weight, looks like," Lavinia gloats to her daughter.

⚜

Every summer, beginning when Dorcas was four, Edgar drove the family to Ocean City, New Jersey, for a week's vacation; Sister went along. They stayed at the Prince of

Wales Inn, several blocks from the boardwalk. Frannie and her family from Philadelphia stayed there, too. Becca was exactly the same age as Dorcas.

The Prince was a plain clapboard hotel, distinguished from other similar hotels by its faded green awnings. The Buchanans took rooms on the top floor, a long climb up four flights of creaking, thinly carpeted stairs, because Lavinia believed those rooms caught the ocean breeze. Dorcas shared a room with Sister until the summer Dorcas was thirteen and Sister announced that she'd decided to stay home.

That summer Dorcas was allowed to room with Becca.

But it turned out to be a week of exquisite torture, because Becca was light years ahead of Dorcas in everything that mattered. Lavinia heard from the anguished Dorcas that Becca had started her periods (Dorcas had not). Becca had let Dorcas read a book called *Frank Talk for Girls* and smirked at Dorcas's deep ignorance. "I've known this stuff for ages," Becca said. This peeved Lavinia when she found out about it. What a snot-brat that Becca was!

By the time the girls reached high school, Becca was applying Pan-Cake makeup and mascara and curling her eyelashes. Becca wedged cotton balls between her toes and painted her toenails. Dressing for the evening stroll on the boardwalk, Becca dabbed White Shoulders on her pulse points and clasped a fine gold ID bracelet around her ankle. She carried a pack of Chesterfields and pretended to smoke. Lavinia watched, dismayed, as Dorcas copied Becca in everything.

Boys hovered like famished seagulls around Becca's beach towel, flocked to the Prince's porch after dinner to joke with her, and struck up conversations with her on the boardwalk. But Dorcas never said one word to her parents that she wanted to go to the Poconos or Wildwood or almost anywhere but Ocean City. How was Lavinia to know that, for Dorcas, the summers had become pure hell?

If she'd known, she might not have persuaded Edgar the summer of 1958 to spend one last family vacation in Ocean City. It was to be a final fling before Dorcas left home to start her teaching job. They planned it for the week of her twenty-second birthday in July.

"Fran wrote me—Becca will be at the shore, too," Lavinia told Dorcas. "She's staying at a boardinghouse and working as a waitress for the summer. You girls will have fun. It'll be the last time you two get to do this, now that Becca's engaged."

Throughout the year Lavinia had received reports from Fran: Becca finding a diamond ring in her champagne glass on New Year's Eve; Becca and Jack announcing their engagement at an Easter brunch; Becca and Jack planning a September wedding. Then Becca herself wrote to Dorcas, asking her to be one of the bridesmaids, and Dorcas accepted.

"You'll have so much to talk about at the beach!" Lavinia told her.

The Buchanans arrived at the Prince of Wales late on a muggy Sunday afternoon and found a note at the desk from Becca: "Jack came down for the weekend. See you at noon tomorrow!" So Dorcas ended up spending her first evening playing cards with her parents.

It was well past noon the next day when Becca came by, dressed in a scanty two-piece number with a boned top that showed off a golden tan. As the two left for the beach—Becca sporting a large straw hat and Dorcas, pale as milk, loaded down with a robe, bathing cap, baby oil, beach towel, and plastic cups to protect her eyes—Lavinia got her first inkling that this trip might not have been such a splendid idea.

Hours later Dorcas returned to the Prince of Wales alone, her skin burned bright pink around the edges of her Lastex bathing suit, her hair matted with sand and salt water. "I guess you two must have had a pretty good time," Lavinia ventured.

Dorcas shrugged. "We did. I guess I lost track of the time. I met a boy and we went swimming." Dorcas grinned at Lavinia. "His name is Alex. He's Hungarian. He used to live in Paris."

CHAPTER 15

Lavinia lets the brass knocker fall three times, pushes open the door, and steps into the chilly hall. "Yoo-hoo!" she hollers, "it's only me!" Dorcas comes out to greet her, bundled in a baggy sweater. "It's like a barn in here," Lavinia complains with a shiver. She peers around. "Any customers?" she stage-whispers, as she does every time. It *is* the middle of winter, after all.

And, as she does every time, Dorcas shakes her head. "Come on in the parlor where it's warmer," she says, although Lavinia knows that even that parlor is an icebox. "Ready for some coffee?"

Lavinia has gotten into the habit of coming by after lunch, unless Dorcas happens to be substituting that day. She likes the idea of Dorcas living close by after all these years, but sometimes it's all she can do to keep her mouth shut about this so-called business. As far as she can tell, Dorcas is the owner, manager, hostess, cook, chambermaid, and—except for Brownie Wilson's relatives at Thanksgiving—sole occupant of the best and only bed-and-breakfast in Juniata. If it weren't for the teaching, it's likely she'd starve. Lavinia wishes Dorcas wouldn't wear that ugly sweater.

In the entrance hall Dorcas has hung a framed map showing the scenic roads that wind through the worn-down mountains and narrow valleys of central Pennsylvania, all highways on their way to someplace else: Harrisburg, for instance, or State College. Morgan House is supposed to appeal to tourists who've wandered off the beaten track, but what if there *are* no tourists? The old Coleman Hotel was boarded up for two years before it was finally turned into senior housing. Green Gables Inn, where Dorcas's wedding reception was held, shut down years ago. That left Mountain View Motel to take in occasional travelers from Altoona, York, King of Prussia.

The situation is hard on Lavinia's nerves.

They have their decaf now in the parlor, where it's perhaps five degrees warmer than in the dining room, but Lavinia keeps her coat on anyway. "I have a favor to ask," she says, stirring a tiny spoonful of sugar into her coffee. "It's my turn to have the girls for our bridge luncheon, and I never know what to feed them. Could you possibly help me out?"

"Be glad to. Leave it to me."

"Wonderful. No vegetable paté, though. No hard biscuits."

"I'll think of something nice."

"I know you will," although she isn't so sure. The coffee warms her, and she slips off her coat, keeping it around her shoulders. Dorcas does make good coffee. "Any news?"

"Actually, yes," Dorcas says cheerily. "I've decided to start serving Sunday brunch, to generate some income and get the place better known around town. If that's successful, I may start doing breakfasts every morning."

Lavinia doesn't know what to make of this latest scheme. You can't say Dorcas isn't trying. She did join the Motel and Hotel Owners Association over in State College, and she took ads in a couple of those glossy tourist magazines. Recently Dorcas told her, "When the weather gets better, I'm going to offer tours of Big Valley, to show visitors some real Amish country. Better than the commercial stuff in Lancaster County."

That might be a good idea. But now, *brunch*?

"Ten ninety-five," Dorcas says.

"Sounds high."

"Cooked to order. Not like those buffets with greasy potatoes and dried-out scrambled eggs."

"Still. Nobody wants to pay eleven dollars for breakfast."

"Brunch. Brunch is different." Dorcas sighs. "We'll see. I'm putting an ad in the *Sentinel.*"

"I'll spread the word," Lavinia promises. "Some people at church might be interested. And the bridge club."

Before she leaves, Lavinia steps into the powder room under the stairway. She flushes the toilet, causing the pipes to rattle, and glares at herself in the mirror. Sagging jowls, chin whiskers, skin like something crumpled up and thrown away—how did she ever get to look so old?

Dorcas is waiting to help her on with her coat. "Be careful," she says as Lavinia sets out for home. As though she might suddenly dart out into traffic like a heedless child.

⁂

On the second Thursday of January, Lavinia prepares to entertain her friends. As soon as she struggles out of bed, and long before Dorcas arrives with the food, Lavinia puts away the painting she's been working on, a nude couple dancing in a stoneyard among carved angels. She locks the painting in the back of the old cedar closet that Rodney made into a storage space. She wonders if he's told Dorcas about it, although he swore he wouldn't.

Two of Lavinia's guests have phoned their regrets—Coey Rothrock is down with a cold, and Marge Kramer says her hill is a sheet of ice. "I'm going to stay put," Marge says. "What are you serving for lunch?"

"I'm not sure," Lavinia says airily. "Dorcas is taking care of it."

"Promise you'll call and tell me all about it," Marge begs. "I think you all gossip more when I'm not there."

Dorcas arrives later than Lavinia wanted her to and helps her open the drop-leaf table and set up a card table and extra chairs. The room is too crowded, but that can't be helped. Lavinia arranges six hemstitched place mats and monogrammed napkins and the good silver and Spode. She sets a crystal goblet at the tip of each knife, and a bread-and-butter plate to the left of the forks. There is a basket lined with an embroidered cloth for the rolls, and a chunk of butter on an antique silver butter dish.

Dorcas leaves a pot of leek soup simmering on the stove, and a warm bean and tuna salad with goat cheese on the counter, with instructions to warm it up just a little before it's served. Lavinia isn't so sure how this strange salad will go over. Beans are supposed to be either hot, like Boston baked beans, or cold, like a three-bean salad, and she's never heard of *tuna* with beans. She's disappointed that Mrs. Putting-on-the-Dog Kramer will miss it, but she counts on the others to rave. She hopes no one complains about gas.

Dorcas leaves before the guests arrive. It takes them a while to get upstairs, since they must come up one by one on the Stair-glider. When their coats and bags have been hung in the closet, only inches from the hidden paintings, and they're settled in chairs that accommodate various back and leg conditions, Lavinia carries out six cocktail glasses clinking on a silver tray. She has a little surprise for the girls that she didn't mention to Dorcas—a pitcher of martinis. "Something to chase away the January blues," she says.

"Oh, you wicked woman!" cries Violet Worley delightedly.

While Lavinia delivers the martinis, Dorrine Laudenslager assumes the role of assistant hostess and carries around a dish of nuts. Not one of those cheap mixes, either, but 100 percent cashews.

"Cheers," says Violet happily, raising her glass. "I feel better already. I might make it through the rest of the winter."

Thanks to the martinis, Lavinia forgets to reheat the bean and tuna salad; no one knows the difference. The soup goes over well. Stella McAllister doesn't know what leeks are, but Esther Bowersox is pleased to explain. "I know," Stella says meanly, "you and Herb had them in New York."

The goat cheese is examined and carefully moved to the side by four of the guests. Nobody mentions gas. Lavinia pours another round of martinis to go with the poached pears that Dorcas left for dessert.

"Tell Dorcas it's all wonderful," says Grace Metzler. "She should open a restaurant."

"Well, I have news for you," Lavinia announces, suddenly remembering. "Starting February 2, she's going to be serving Sunday brunch. Be sure to tell all your friends." Lavinia considers whether she should mention the price. "Cooked to order, too," she says. "Ten ninety-five."

"That's high," Dorrine says.

"You have to pay for quality," Lavinia reminds her. "Fresh orange juice, all you want. No dried-up scrambled eggs."

"Has she had much business in overnight guests?" Violet asks.

Lavinia wishes she had a good answer for this one. "I don't honestly know how that's going," she fibs, "but Dorcas isn't worried. She has lots of ideas."

"You know," says Esther, who was Dorcas's Latin teacher in high school, "I'm just surprised that Dorcas hasn't remarried. Such a smart, attractive girl, I always thought once she got a man, she'd hang on to him."

Lavinia stiffens at the implied criticism.

"Well, she might just have had enough of men," Violet suggests. "I'd never marry again. Would you?"

"That's because you never liked sex," says Grace.

"Who says I didn't like sex?" Violet demands.

Stella, who appears to be slightly looped, gazes around and asks loudly, "Do you remember the first time you had it?"

Lavinia, concerned about the turn of the conversation, levers herself up out of her chair. "Would anyone care for coffee? Or tea?"

"No, thanks," says Violet. "But a little more gin would be nice."

"I'm all out," Lavinia lies.

"Well, then, coffee will be fine."

Fortunately, the pot is already set up, and all she has to do is turn it on. She doesn't want to be out of the room if the talk gets completely out of hand. Or to miss anything.

Stella repeats her question: "Do you remember when you lost your precious pearl?"

"I never lost mine," says Grace. "I gave it away."

They howl with laughter and slap their rickety knees.

"Well, the rest of you may be losing your memories," Esther says, "but I certainly haven't. I will *never* forget the first time I saw Herb's Thing when it turned into a throbbing monster. I ran screaming out of our hotel bedroom and locked myself in the bathroom."

"Men are so *ugly* down there," Violet says, shuddering. "I'd sure hate to run around with a thing like that between my legs."

Dorrine gasps and Stella erupts in giggles. Lavinia rushes to get the coffee.

The sight of Edgar's male organ was no shock when it made its first bold appearance in a hotel room on the way to Niagara Falls. To her shame, all she'd been able to think of at that moment was Nicholas. Edgar believed it was passion for him that caused her murmurs and cries that night, but it was Nicholas. It was always Nicholas. She is thinking of Nicholas and Brother Giovanni now when she tells her guests, "I think they're magnificent."

"Oh, you *would*!" Stella squeals, flapping her hand.

CHAPTER 16

After several months of working almost daily on her memoirs, Lavinia has covered the early years of her life, the parts she considers most interesting. It's going much slower than she expected, and she hasn't yet begun to transfer what she has written from the school notebook into the memoir book.

Mornings, after she's dressed and has breakfast and watches a half hour or so of *Good Morning America,* she sits down at her desk with a cup of coffee and a cigarette and rereads what she wrote the day before. That starts her thinking back, and when she glances at the clock again, she realizes that the morning is gone and she should get herself together and have some lunch and then run on over to see how Dorcas is getting along.

Once Lavinia has gotten past the chapter about Nicholas, which is distressing, she plods through her senior year—the year Mama died—and her graduation from high school and how she begged Pop to let her go to Philadelphia to study acting and voice. She wanted a ca-

reer on the stage, but he wanted her at home, and naturally he won.

Young men came courting, but all of them bored her to
distraction. How could any of those boys compare with a
man like Nicholas! The years passed quickly. Maybe, she
thought, she'd end up an old maid like Sister. The idea
didn't bother her.

Not long after her twenty-third birthday, Pop took her
for a drive. They went out by the stoneyard, rattling over
the ruts of the very same road where a half dozen summers
before she had ridden her bicycle almost every night to
meet Nicholas. Through a cloud of cigar smoke Pop told
her that he wanted her to think about marrying Edgar
Buchanan.

A picture of the young Edgar comes to Lavinia's mind:
a man of medium height and medium build with a kind,
unremarkable face, blue-gray eyes, and straight brown hair
with a small, gleaming bald spot. *But,* she thinks now, *he
was not really so young then.* He was thirty-two, nine years
older than she.

Edgar had been working for Juniata Marble and Granite since Lavinia was in grammar school, starting at the bot-
tom as a salesman and working his way up to manager.
Lavinia had been only dimly aware of him. She was in love
with Nicholas.

"Here's the thing, Lavinia," Pop said in his usual blunt
way. "I want Edgar to take over the business after I'm gone.
He's the only one can do it. Martha's and Kitty's husbands
aren't worth poop, and I want to see the business passed
on. I'd like to see *you* have it, but it's not a woman's business. Next best thing is to see you married to a man that
knows what to do with it. That man is Edgar Buchanan. He
likes you fine, he's already told me that, and I believe he'd

take good care of you." Pop threw her a hard glance. "Could have done far worse, in my opinion." She kept her face a perfect blank. "Nobody's going to force you to do anything. All I'm asking is you think about it."

"All right," Lavinia said, feeling a net drop weightlessly around her. "Tell Edgar to call me."

Edgar called. On Saturday evening he picked her up in his Ford roadster and took her to a movie. He reached for her hand. Edgar's palm was clammy, but she put that down to nerves and let him weave his fingers through hers. "Thank you, Lavinia," he said at the end of the evening, after they'd stopped for ice cream. He made a little bow. She gazed at his bald spot and murmured, "Thank you, Edgar."

On Monday he asked her to go out the following Saturday. It was the same the week after that. Edgar had a nice baritone voice and knew the words to all the popular songs: "Don't Blame Me." "Sweet Sue." He liked to sing while he drove. She sang with him, and they'd harmonize.

When, after six months, he asked her to marry him, she said yes, although she wasn't in love with him. She really didn't expect to be.

It was a small June wedding, just their families and a few close friends. After the ceremony they all went for lunch at the new Coleman Hotel. Lavinia unpinned her corsage and tossed it to Sister, and she and Edgar left for Niagara Falls.

"If you hadn't married him, I would have," Sister said years later, that night on the porch after she'd confessed to telling Pop about Nicholas. Lavinia remembers the conversation clearly.

"You just said you were in love with Nicholas. I didn't know you were in love with Edgar, too," she had replied sharply. "It must have been a habit of yours." She was dying for a cigarette; there was a pack of Chesterfields in the pocket of her housecoat, but Sister didn't like it when Lavinia smoked.

"I'm not saying I was in love with Edgar. I'm just saying one of us in the family had to marry him, because Pop was going to turn the business over to him. I'd known Edgar for a long time—we were almost the same age. But Pop wanted you married. He never trusted you after he found out about you and Nicholas."

"After *you* told him about Nicholas!" Lavinia decided to have a cigarette anyhow. She tapped one out of the pack. Then she lit it deliberately with the silver lighter Edgar had given her for an anniversary present and blew smoke straight at Sister.

CHAPTER 17

A week after the bridge luncheon, Coey Rothrock drops by Lavinia's apartment, uninvited, while Lavinia is writing in her notebook. Coey is the only one of Lavinia's friends who comes by any old time and plunks herself down. As though Lavinia has nothing better to do than drop everything and entertain her.

"Over your cold?" Lavinia asks as Coey ascends on the Stair-glider. So far she's made it through the winter without one, knock on wood, and she doesn't want one now.

"Oh yes," Coey says. "I'm fit as a fiddle."

Lavinia takes Coey's coat with the fur trim. It's the same one she's been wearing for the last thirty years, Lavinia notices, since Wasserman's went out of business. "Can I get you a cup of coffee?"

"I hear you served martinis for lunch last week," Coey says with a cute smile.

"Indeed I did," Lavinia says. "And those girls drank up gin like it was going out of style. Didn't leave me a drop!"

"Well, then, tea would be nice. Especially if you have lemon. I always take lemon in my tea."

Once they're settled, Coey begins to question Lavinia. "Marge says she heard from Violet that your food was delish."

"Dorcas did it for me," Lavinia brags, but Coey already knows that. She also knows that Dorcas is going to be charging ten ninety-five for her Sunday breakfast.

"Brunch," Lavinia explains. "Brunch is much more elaborate than breakfast. And then she might start serving regular breakfasts during the week. Less fancy." *Cheaper, too, I hope.*

"Just between you and me and the deep blue sea," Coey says conspiratorially, leaning close, "how is Dorcas doing?"

"Why, she's doing just fine! It takes time to get a business on its feet."

"I don't mean the business, necessarily." Coey takes the plastic lemon, which is all Lavinia has to offer, and squirts juice into her tea. "I just wondered if she doesn't find life here lonely. Being on her own and all."

Lavinia has wondered the same thing, but it annoys her that Coey is asking the question. "I really don't think that's any of my business." *Or yours.*

Coey fishes a packet of sugar substitute out of her purse and taps the powder into her tea. "I was wondering if she might not be interested in Rodney Benner."

What outrageous nonsense, Lavinia thinks. She has known Coey Rothrock for years, since she was Coey Vaughn and didn't have a pot to piss in, and Coey has never known when to keep her mouth shut.

"I can't imagine anything of the kind," Lavinia says, although, as a matter of fact, she can. She often sees Rod sitting alone at the counter at the Trolley Stop, and she has to admit that he's a nice-looking man. Honest, too. The kind a woman would be attracted to. But—and she's not about to say any of this to Coey—Rodney is not Dorcas's type; Dorcas has always gone for more exotic types, oddballs really, and Rodney is just a nice local boy. She changes the subject. "By the way, isn't the next bridge luncheon at your house?"

"Yes, it is, and it's Marge's birthday," Coey says and sets down her cup and saucer. "You don't suppose Dorcas would be willing to help me out? I'd pay her whatever she asks."

Lavinia doesn't think much of this idea. After all, Dorcas is her ace in the hole, and if everybody starts to use her, Lavinia will have no advantage. Still, Dorcas might need the money. "You'll have to discuss that with her," she says.

It seems as though Coey will never leave, but when she finally does, Lavinia pulls out her notebook, opens to a clean page, and prints DORCAS across the top.

My daughter was born at 5 A.M. on the morning of July 29, 1936, after a long, difficult delivery. I thought sure I was going to split down the middle and die. The doctor told Edgar that another pregnancy might kill me and another delivery surely would. Edgar was so let down—he always wanted a son.

We named her Dorcas, for Edgar's mother, and Edna, for mine.

In looks, Dorcas took after Edgar right from the start. The only thing she got from Lavinia was her blue eyes. Her "Juniata blues," Edgar called them.

Lavinia was always afraid of spoiling Dorcas, such an easy thing to do with an only child, so Lavinia was the one to say no, while it seemed that Edgar let her have her own way. Even worse, Sister indulged Dorcas in subtle—sometimes, Lavinia thought, sneaky—ways.

Oh, Dorcas was bright enough, an A student, but she wasn't *clever*—not clever enough to hide her brains from the boys. Lavinia, who always had her pick of sweethearts, worried about Dorcas as she plowed headlong into her high school years. There was the O'Brien boy, and one or two others, but none that Lavinia considered much of a bargain.

"Lord knows *who* she'll end up with," Lavinia fretted often to Edgar. "You know how she is."

The one she'd ended up with was Alex, with his foreign clothes and foreign put-on manners and that accent! "An oddball, if I ever saw one," Lavinia complained to Edgar.

"If that's who she has her heart set on, so be it. I'm not going to interfere, and neither are you." His tone shocked Lavinia, but she said no more.

Lavinia had never discussed sex with Dorcas. That was something that must be figured out privately, between husband and wife. The only thing a girl needed to know about sex was that she must avoid it at all costs until the wedding band was on her finger. The very idea that Dorcas might get herself into a situation like Lavinia's with Nicholas made her faint with alarm.

Alex and Dorcas got married, and more than half a dozen years went by with no sign of a baby. Could something be wrong? Lavinia worried but said nothing.

Then, miraculously, Dorcas got pregnant. She never looked better, happier, more glowing than when she was carrying Sasha. No baby ever received a more ecstatic welcome into the world than little Alexandra Lavinia. Lavinia was pleased as punch to have the child named for her, although how they got Sasha out of Alexandra, Lavinia never could figure out.

If ever there was a Daddy's girl, it was Sasha. Alex adored her, just the way Edgar had always doted on Dorcas. Lavinia hoped there would be another, perhaps a boy next time. But there wasn't. Now Dorcas, too, would bring up an only child, a daughter. Now she'd find out it wasn't so easy.

And then, with no warning whatsoever and no explanation that made an iota of sense to Lavinia, the marriage ended.

As Lavinia tries to set down the important things about Dorcas, the evening on the porch with Sister comes back to her with disturbing clarity.

"How is Dorcas?" Sister had asked. "And Sasha?"

"They're all fine. Sasha is as cute as can be. Alex works too hard. He's not home much—Dorcas complains about that."

Sister smoothed her dress over her knees. She was wearing thick hose, as she always did, and probably an old-fashioned corset, too, even in the heat of summer.

"I honestly thought she'd have left him by now," Sister said, "but I imagine she stays because of Sasha. She wasn't really in love with Alex when she married him, you know."

One revelation after another had tumbled out in the course of that one evening, and Lavinia could not stand to hear any more. "Well, of course I knew, Sister," Lavinia lied smoothly. She had to urinate, but this was no time to get up and walk away. "Most of us don't end up marrying someone we're head over heels in love with." She was thinking of Nicholas. "I believe Dorcas cares for Alex, and he cares for her."

Sister seemed to know everyone's secrets, but who knew Sister's? She was the one who stayed at home, taking care of Mama, and after Mama died, stayed on to keep house for Lavinia and Pop. Then Lavinia married, and after Pop died some ten years later, Sister was alone. Still, Lavinia thought, she seemed contented with her life.

But maybe she wasn't after all, Lavinia thinks now. Maybe Sister was in love with Edgar all those years and never let on. And Edgar—what about him? Did he know about Sister's feelings? Is it even possible that Edgar harbored some desire for Sister? Lavinia can't guess. Edgar was another one who'd kept his own counsel. It's galling to imagine that Sister might have known more about Dorcas than Lavinia did—the worst betrayal of all.

It is late afternoon, nearly dark outside, when Lavinia slaps shut her notebook and pushes herself stiffly to her feet. There's always somebody telling her something she doesn't want to hear.

PART III

DORCAS

CHAPTER 18

Dorcas presents an ambitious brunch menu: eggs Benedict, pecan waffles with real maple syrup, ham and potato omelet, salmon quiche. She opens the dining room table and sets up two tables of four in the parlor. She advertises the hours from eleven to one-thirty, remembering that people in Juniata like to eat early but forgetting that nobody will arrive until after church lets out.

She has hired Bonnie Gutshall, daughter of the loan officer from the bank, to help. Bonnie appears with fake fingernails and a tight skirt so short that it barely covers her butt. Dorcas struggles in the kitchen to keep up. She hadn't realized how hard it is to poach eggs to order.

Rootie comes, and so does Marlene Benner with her sister from Williamsport. Dorcas wonders if Rod will show up. She hasn't seen him since before Christmas, when he finished the two attic rooms.

The day he began work on the third floor, Rod brought down a rusted metal box he found hidden in the rafters. Inside the box was a crumbling sheet of paper, the ink faded to brown. It was dated November 14, 1873.

This indenture witnesseth that Aaron Vincent of the City of Juniata doth put and bind out his daughter Caroline Vincent as an apprentice to William A. Morgan to learn the art and mystery of housekeeping.

"'The art and mystery of housekeeping,'" Rod said, shaking his head. "Enough to make you cry."

"William Morgan promised to teach her to 'read, write and cipher,'" Dorcas said, handling the document gingerly. "At the end of seven years, she'd get half a dozen chairs, a bed, a bureau, and a table. I hope he treated her well."

"I'll do some checking and see what I can find out about her," Rod promised, "soon as I finish this job."

The week before Christmas, the attic rooms were done. Dorcas was decorating a Scotch pine in the parlor when Rod stopped by to submit his final bill. "Well, listen, Dorcas," he said, pocketing the check, "if there's anything else you need, give me a holler."

"I will." She lifted a silver ornament from the box. "And you'll let me know if you find out anything about Caroline Vincent?"

The metal hook was missing from the ornament, replaced years earlier with a loop of red string. Suddenly, it slipped out of her hands and exploded as it hit the floor, scattering shards of silvery glass. "Oh, *damn!*" Dorcas cried. "I bought these for Sasha's first Christmas. It's just about all that's left of her childhood." Her throat felt gritty.

Rod stooped to help her clean it up. "Might be nice to have a fire," he said, "to cheer you up." Without waiting for a reply, he began arranging kindling and logs. Dorcas brought two beers from the refrigerator. She sat on the sofa, he took the armchair, and together they watched the fire.

On Christmas Eve, as Dorcas was preparing to leave for Lavinia's, Rod appeared at the door and handed her a small, square box. "Merry Christmas," he said.

Dorcas lifted the lid; inside was a tree ornament, red, with MORGAN HOUSE 1870 lettered on it in gold. "Thought you needed to start a new tradition," he said.

She hugged him, pressing her nose against his shoulder, murmuring, "Thank you, thank you."

Rod stepped back and took her face in his hands. "Could've sworn there was some mistletoe around here somewhere," he said gruffly, but didn't kiss her. That was over a month ago. He hasn't been around since.

"I don't suppose you want my advice," Lavinia whispers to Dorcas after the brunch, "but here it is anyway: Do something about Bonnie. Her fingernails are enough to ruin anybody's appetite. And tell her not to bend over."

Dorcas is rubbing oil into a water mark on the dining room table when Rod taps at the backdoor. "I came by to see how it went," he says. "The brunch."

"All right, I guess, for a first time. Want some coffee?"

According to Rootie, Rod has moved out of the room he'd rented and into an apartment. "Marlene is still calling it a trial separation," Rootie reported, "but I'd say the verdict is already in." She added, "If Marlene and I weren't friends, I'd definitely be putting the moves on that guy."

Dorcas pours two cups and sets them on the kitchen table. Rod asks, "Think you made a profit today?"

Dorcas shrugs. "After I paid Bonnie and figured in my other costs, I cleared about fifty dollars. But," she says, with an optimism that sounds false in her own ears, "if it catches on, I may start serving breakfasts during the week."

He reaches across the table and pats her hand. "You're a hard worker," he says. "Tell you what. I've got a place of my own now, with a kitchen. Baking bread's kind of a hobby. I could make you some sticky buns every week, if you wanted me to."

They work out a deal: two dozen sticky buns delivered warm each Sunday, in exchange for brunch. Within a month, Dorcas has cut her Sunday menu choices to three; Bonnie stays in the kitchen, long nails out of sight. Rod's sticky buns are a hit.

Sometimes, before he leaves, Rod helps clean up; afterward, they sit and talk. He tells her about his new project, remodeling a house for the historical society. "I got the job because of you—somebody at your open house liked my work. The Stamms? I may be asking you for advice. Mrs. Stamm knows a lot, but she doesn't know squat about color."

Occasionally they talk about their previous lives. Dorcas is startled when Rod tells her about taking a bus to Selma, Alabama, in 1965 for the civil rights march to Montgomery. "Did you take part in any of the protests?" he asks.

She shakes her head, no. Why hadn't she? Too self-centered, she thinks now, ruefully, but she puts the blame on Alex. "My husband was afraid for me to get involved."

Rod smiles knowingly. "Marlene wasn't too happy, either, about me leaving her with the kids."

Dorcas begins serving simple breakfasts five mornings a week and starts taking reservations for the brunches; all three sittings on Easter are fully booked. But Morgan House has had no overnight guests, and the bright rooms sit empty, the fireplaces cold.

※

Rod comes by on a Sunday afternoon and finishes off the sweet pepper frittata. She has framed the document of indenture that he found in the attic, and he hangs it for her in the hall at the foot of the stairs. "I've been doing some research on this Caroline Vincent girl," he says. "I want you to come to the cemetery with me."

Dorcas likes the perspective of sitting up high in the front seat of Rod's truck. "If you haven't been to the genealogical library in the old courthouse, you should check it out," Rod tells her. "Your William Alfred Morgan owned an iron furnace in Juniata and mines all over the county. Laborers dug it out by hand and hauled it to the furnace. According to the records I found, Caroline's father, Aaron Vincent, was a miner. Hard, dirty work, low wages. Apprenticing his daughter to the boss probably seemed like a good idea at the time."

"You'd make a good detective," she says.

"I told you—I like history."

They drive to the oldest part of the cemetery, which Dorcas has never seen on her many trips here. Rod leads her to a small headstone tipped at an angle. The ground is soggy, and there are crusty patches of snow in shaded spots. Dorcas crouches down to read the worn letters: *Caroline Vincent, Dau. of Aaron and Eliz. Vincent. Born Oct 4, 1863. Died Mar 31, 1875.*

"The paper you found was dated 1873. She was only ten when she went to live with the Morgans!" Dorcas exclaims. "And eleven when she died. Somehow I wish you hadn't found this. I'd rather think that she collected her bed and bureau and her table and chairs, married a good man, and lived a happy life."

"I'm sorry," Rod says. "I thought you'd be interested."

"I am. I just feel bad for her, that's all. Do you have any idea what she died from?"

"I can probably find out. They've got old newspapers on microfiche. I could see if there were any epidemics."

"Oh, I hope the Morgans were good to her!" Dorcas exclaims.

For days after the trip to the cemetery, Dorcas can't get the fate of Caroline Vincent out of her mind. Rod has a report when he delivers the next batch of sticky buns. "She fell through the ice on the river and drowned."

Dorcas's throat tightens and she begins to cry, as though she'd actually known Caroline. Rod awkwardly grips her shoulder, pats her back. She wipes her eyes. "We need to talk," she says, "about putting in a garden."

❧

Two middle-aged Englishwomen, traveling across America by train, climb off the westbound Chicago Limited and take a taxi from the depot to the center of Juniata. They wander into the Trolley Stop with their old-fashioned rucksacks, inquiring after a place to stay. Lavinia is there. Wanda phones Dorcas.

"Your village does remind me of Switzerland!" gurgles one, as Dorcas drives them through town. She has gingery hair and an overbite. "Certain parts, of course," adds the thinner, more reserved one.

The Englishwomen choose to stay in the Lily of the Valley Room with the balcony overlooking what will become the garden. Dorcas plans to call it "Caroline's Garden," and Rod has promised to send Charlie to work on it as soon as the ground warms up. Dorcas makes them tea the English way, rinsing the pot with hot water before she steeps the tea. She bakes them scones. She drives them up to Big Valley to view the neat Amish farms and takes them to see Lavinia's Amish paintings. They fall in love with Lavinia, who serves them martinis—doubles, very dry. On their last day, Dorcas waits with them at the depot until the train arrives, two hours late.

Then Debbie Larber, wife of Lavinia's attorney, calls to inquire if Dorcas does weddings. "Our daughter has decided to get married in June," says Debbie. "Just a small, intimate affair. We thought it would be nice to have it at your place. And put up some of the members of the wedding party for the weekend."

Dorcas opens her big black reservation book and scans the empty pages. "Fortunately," she says, "the weekend you want is free."

❧

Two days after Mother's Day Dorcas and Lavinia carry their coffee outside to inspect Charlie's progress on Caroline's Garden. The rough work has been done: beds laid out, paths installed, trellises built. Inside, the phone rings. It's Sasha.

"Mom?" Sasha says, and Dorcas immediately recognizes that tearful quaver in her voice. Panic grabs her by the throat, as it has since the day Sasha was born.

"Sasha, what's wrong?"

Sasha struggles with a sob. "It's Daddy."

"Alex? What about him?" Her child is safe, and Dorcas allows herself to relax.

"Ellen just called," Sasha says. "He's really sick, Mom. He has lung cancer. Ellen says he might not have long, and I should come."

"Oh Sasha, I'm so sorry!" Dorcas leans her forehead against the wall. Bit by bit she coaxes out the information. They've begun aggressive chemotherapy, but the cancer has already spread to Alex's spine. A CAT scan of the brain is scheduled; the signs are ominous.

Water rattles the pipes, and the door of the powder room opens. Lavinia stands in the doorway, hands and feet braced, as though she expects an earthquake. Dorcas covers the mouthpiece with her hand and tells her mother, "Alex has cancer." She speaks again into the phone. "How long, Sasha? Do they have any idea? Did Ellen say?"

"I'm not sure. A few weeks, maybe. For some reason he didn't want me to know." Dorcas hears her blow her nose. "I want to go see him soon as I can work it out," Sasha says wetly. "So I was wondering, could I stop there on the way? To see you and Lovey?"

"You know I'd love to have you. Your grandmother and I both would."

Lavinia waits until Dorcas hangs up and listens to the details. "I *thought* something must be wrong when I didn't get a plant at Easter!" she says.

⁂

On the day they met, Alex grabbed Dorcas's hand and ran with her into the ocean. When they came out of the water, Becca had left for work, but Alex's cousin, Toby, lay stretched out on the hot sand. He was reading Hemingway, Dorcas noticed. They lay down beside him, and while the sun coasted across the milky sky, the three of them talked.

Without Becca, Dorcas felt both more animated and more relaxed. There was so much she wanted to ask them! She'd never met anybody from Hungary before, or anybody who'd been forced to flee his homeland because of war and politics. Toby spoke several languages and gave her a sample—"You have beautiful blue eyes"—translated into French, Spanish, Italian, German, and Hungarian.

Alex was in love with everything about the U.S., he said, "Except the food." He had nothing but scorn for American bread, Velveeta cheese, peanut butter, and overdone meat. Toby didn't criticize, merely mentioning that he always enjoyed a glass of wine with dinner and sometimes with lunch, too. "A meal without wine is like a day without sunshine."

Of the two—sandy-haired, blue-eyed Alex and dark-haired Toby with eyes like Hershey kisses—she thought Toby was better-looking and more mysterious. But it was Alex who had asked her to swim, Alex who wanted *her*.

"I'm afraid you will be burned," Alex said late in the afternoon, eyeing her cooking flesh.

Her skin was already tingling. In a few days it would blister, and then the dead skin would come off in shreds. "I never seem to do things in stages," she said. "All or nothing."

At dinner her mother wanted to know more about "the Hungarians," but Dorcas told her as little as possible, detouring instead to describe Becca's wedding plans. She realized how dull this food would seem to the two boys— canned fruit cocktail, baked ham, wax beans, macaroni and cheese. She drank her milk resentfully.

Afterward, dressed in what she believed was her sexiest outfit, a black silk sheath with a short white jacket, she announced that she planned to stroll on the boardwalk until Becca finished work.

"Alone?" her mother asked.

God! "Mother, I'll be twenty-two in a few days."

Conscious of the movement of her hips inside the silk sheath, Dorcas sauntered past the amusement arcade where Alex and his cousin worked. To kill time, she watched the saltwater taffy machine at Shriver's. In a souvenir shop she bought a compact decorated with little seashells for Sister. She peered into the Clam Shack and spotted Becca, wearing a perky green uniform and balancing a tray.

She saved until last the dimly lit cubbyhole where an old man hunched over a little flame and worked threads of molten glass into delicate miniature figures—a full-rigged sailing ship barely three inches high, a bright-colored parrot in a tiny cage. Every summer, Dorcas bought a piece or two for her collection. Now her attention was drawn to a string quartet, four little figures in tailcoats, their chairs, their music stands, and their instruments all made of impossibly fine glass filaments. She decided to buy the cellist.

The fragile musician wrapped in wads of cotton, Dorcas strolled back to the arcade. Her new white pumps were rubbing blisters on her heels. The straps of her bra gnawed her sunburned shoulders. If Becca were there, they would laugh and talk, and every laugh, every gesture, would be calculated for the boys' benefit. She decided not to play miniature golf or ride the Ferris wheel; that was just too obvious. She bought a box of popcorn and sat down across from the arcade, watching for Toby.

The ticket seller closed the wooden shutter, the Ferris wheel slowed and stopped, the music on the merry-go-round fell silent, the lights blinked out, but no sign of Toby. Then Alex appeared. In his white uniform Alex wasn't as sexy as his cousin in brief bathing trunks, but he was definitely good-looking.

"I'm waiting for Becca," she said, a half-truth.

"My cousin is taking her for coffee," Alex said. "I hoped you were waiting for me."

What was I waiting for? Dorcas wonders now. *Romance, probably. Any kind of excitement.*

Alex led her down the steps and onto the empty beach. The tide was out. Dorcas took off her shoes, a huge relief, and they walked on the cool, damp sand. After a tantalizing delay, he kissed her, his tongue searching, his body tight against hers. "Come with me," he said. "I know a place."

She followed him through a scrim of beach grass and ducked into the murky world beneath the boardwalk. Chevrons of light sliced between the wooden planks. Alex took off his white shirt and spread it on the sand for her. Much sexier without the shirt. "Pleasant, is it not?" he asked. "A secret hideaway." Footsteps thumped above their heads and waves boomed a few yards away.

Before Dorcas started high school, Lavinia's lectures had begun: "The very worst thing a girl can do to her parents is to go all the way and get herself in trouble. If you're ever tempted, just think of how that would hurt your father and me."

The lectures had their effect. Even as Alex's tongue teased her nipples and his fingers found the crotch of her cotton underpants, Dorcas thought guiltily of her mother. But by the time they crept out from beneath the boardwalk much later that night, Dorcas had gone farther with Alex in one evening than she had in all her other make-out sessions. Her silk sheath was a wrinkled mess, and she'd lost a button; she'd have to take it to the cleaners herself.

Each afternoon that week Dorcas hurried to the beach to meet Becca and Alex and Toby. Listening to the Hungarians, she discovered more things that she must learn to do: play chess, speak a foreign language fluently, ski both downhill and slalom. She was grateful that she knew how to dance, because right there on the beach Alex broke into an enthusiastic lindy, and she managed to keep up. Becca looked disapproving and later offered a bit of advice: "Everyone was staring. Boys don't like girls who attract attention to themselves."

"It was his idea," Dorcas said defiantly.

She wished, though, that it had been Toby. Why wasn't it? Toby looked at her as though he wanted her, but it was always Alex who made the first move.

On their last evening, Alex crouched above her, until her thighs, of their own accord, opened wider, and his tongue caressed the spot between her legs that she'd never really understood. Dizzy with desire and simultaneously frantic with fear, she feebly pushed him away. "Dorcas," he whispered, "you won't get pregnant and you'll still be a virgin. I would never harm you. I want to please you. Trust me." She did, and let go.

Then he showed her how to take his penis in her mouth. Afterward he taught her the Latin words for what they had done.

"Cunnilingus," she murmured. "Fellatio." She believed that she should be shocked, but she wasn't. She wondered if Becca knew about this. If her mother did.

She pictures the young Alex of that long-ago summer. And now he's ill, dying of cancer. *I gave in too quickly*, she thinks. *I didn't know enough then to wait for what I really wanted.*

CHAPTER 19

"Are they here yet?"

It's Lavinia, phoning for the third time, even though Dorcas promised she'd let her know the minute Sasha and her friend arrived. "Not yet," Dorcas says.

"You don't suppose something's happened."

"When she called last night, she said they'd probably get in around noon if they got an early enough start. I'm sure she'd let us know if there's a problem."

"Well, now you know what it's like. All those times I waited and *waited* for a phone call from you. A simple phone call was all I asked."

Dorcas's head is throbbing, despite four aspirin. Since Sasha's first call ten days ago with news of Alex's illness, Dorcas has awakened every morning at 3:00 A.M., unable to go back to sleep. Their visits in the past—Sasha's trips back east, Dorcas's trips to California—haven't always turned out the way she hoped, the way she believed they should, and this visit carries extra burdens. Alex's illness clouds judgment, distorts feeling, for both of them.

"Sasha, don't you think it would be better to fly?" she'd asked when Sasha told her she'd decided to drive. "It's such a long way, and you'll be under a lot of stress."

But even as she asked the question, Dorcas knew she didn't have the cash for plane fare. She's dangling by a slender, frayed thread, struggling to keep Morgan House going and already so deeply in debt to Lavinia that she can't bear to ask for another penny. But Lavinia might offer to pay for it, if Sasha asked her, and Dorcas suggests that.

"I think it's better this way, Mom," Sasha was saying. "Michelle's driving, we're using her truck, so I won't have to do it alone. Besides, I need time to get my head together."

It seems insane. Why would Sasha want to drive? And in a *truck*? Who is this Michelle, who can afford to take time off to drive across the country to visit a housemate's mother and grandmother and dying father and then drive back again?

Sasha was weeping audibly. "Mom? Do you think you could go with us to Connecticut? To see Daddy? Because I don't think I can handle this without you."

Dorcas hesitated. "We'll talk about it, Sasha. Just come, and then we'll figure it out."

Beginning Sunday, the guest rooms on the second floor have been reserved by a historical group touring nineteenth-century iron furnaces. After the historians leave, a large family is booked for the following weekend. It's the busiest she's been since she opened. When Rootie came by for breakfast, as she sometimes did on her way to the library, Dorcas laid out her problem.

"Simple," said Rootie. "Hire me to run Morgan House while you're away. I've always wanted to do something like this. Dave owes me vacation time. I can handle it for a week."

"It's complicated," Dorcas argued. "There's a lot to do. You'll have to cook and serve breakfast, they'll expect fresh orange juice, you have to get the beds made and the bathrooms cleaned, people tend to arrive at odd times—"

"I can manage," Rootie insisted. "I'm good at organizing."

"Then there's Sunday brunches," Dorcas continued doggedly.

"Maybe I could ask Rod to help on Sunday. He'll be bringing the sticky buns, right?"

There was something in Rootie's voice that alerted Dorcas: Had Rootie decided to put the moves on him after all? Dorcas thought of Rod's habit of coming to eat brunch leftovers and talk about his projects. Of the friendship that's grown deeper since their discovery of Caroline Vincent.

"Look," Rootie said with a touch of impatience, "just make me some lists, take your trip, and don't worry about it."

❧

But this trip is not something she wants to do. She hasn't been comfortable around Alex for years, and she isn't good at saying good-bye. When her father died, they'd never really said the final words.

She worries about the practical matters, like how they're going to travel. Will the three of them ride in her Honda or in Michelle's truck? And where will they stay? Maybe Barbara knows of a place that isn't too expensive, although almost everything in Fairfield County is. It will seem odd, staying in a motel in the town where she lived for so many years.

In April 1959 Alex presented Dorcas with a ring that had belonged to his mother. A garnet surrounded by tiny diamonds, it was a little old-fashioned for Dorcas's taste, but it proved to Lavinia that Dorcas's future husband was more than a rootless refugee. Edgar loved to torment her with references to Count Dracula, who was the only Hungarian he could name.

"Anything new from the count?" her father would tease. "Be sure to get the name of his dentist."

Dorcas was positive she had good reasons for marrying Alex. Because he was intelligent and good-looking and three inches taller than she was so she could wear heels. Because he'd taken her by the hand and led her into the water, and because they had slept together and she was no longer a virgin. Because now she would not have to worry about finding a husband, or about disgracing her parents if she got pregnant.

For the first weeks after her wedding, Dorcas gave herself up to the blissful languor of marriage. She could fill a whole day with straightening up their new apartment after early morning sex and breakfast, hauling the laundry down to the basement, and fixing complicated but not very good meals for the two of them. Once a week she kept the VW Bug to run errands. Once a week she scrubbed, vacuumed and dusted. On weekends they drove up to Candlewood Lake with a picnic.

She had decided not to continue teaching, and at the end of the summer, she answered a newspaper ad for a job at Leo Hamilton and Associates, an advertising agency. There were no associates, just Leo, and her job was to answer the phone, type letters, file papers, make coffee. In her mind it was temporary, a year or so until she and Alex started a family. She began composing Leo's letters rather than merely typing up his scrawled longhand. He gave her a brochure to rewrite for a company that imported sewing machines. A golfing magazine hired Hamilton and Associates to prepare a series of promotion pieces; Dorcas was given the assignment and a raise. She opened a bank account in her own name, initiating the first real fight she and Alex had, and she backed down. They deposited her paycheck in a savings account for a house and stopped using a diaphragm. But months went by, and she didn't get pregnant.

Lavinia never asked questions, although it must have nearly choked her to maintain that silence. Dorcas checked with a gynecologist, who assured her that she was in fine shape. "When the time is right, it'll happen," the doctor said, patting her knee. "Meanwhile, my advice is, relax and enjoy it."

Dorcas and Becca kept in touch via long, slyly boastful letters. Dorcas heard all about Becca's darling little girl, Ashley, and about Jack's promotions and their new house. Dorcas retaliated with a Christmas letter that transformed her job at Hamilton into something exciting and glamorous. "We're planning a vacation in Europe," she wrote. "To visit Alex's family."

Then, in January, Edgar was diagnosed with cancer. He hadn't mentioned any problems when they had talked on the phone; Lavinia called back later, when Edgar was out of the house, to tell Dorcas that he was scheduled for surgery. The surgeon removed a section of colon, examined his diseased liver, and advised them to hope for the best. Alex and Dorcas postponed their trip and never did get around to taking it.

❧

Every few minutes Dorcas hurries to the parlor window and peers through the lace curtain at the empty street. She checks again just as a red pickup with California plates slows and stops. For a moment she hesitates and watches through the curtain.

The driver is the first to emerge, a tall, angular woman with short-cropped brown hair. She stands in the street with her hands on her thin hips and arches her back, squinting up at the house. Michelle.

Finally Sasha climbs out. She flashes a grin toward the curtained parlor window, as though she knows that Dorcas is there, watching. As they straggle up the front walk, Dorcas's attention centers on Sasha, in jeans, red socks, a man's shirt. She's let her hair grow long and pulls it back in a straggly twist. She rolls like a sailor coming off a ship after months at sea.

Dorcas rushes to fling open the door, relieved that they've arrived safely. She has to remind herself that she's not the focus of the journey. They're here because of Alex, and his approaching death is the reason they've driven all the way across the country.

Sasha ambles toward her, the grin still wide, and Dorcas hugs her hard. Michelle stalls Dorcas with a handshake and keeps her distance, seeming to measure her with aloof green eyes, like a person who expects rejection, takes it for granted.

"Lovey's coming over for supper," Dorcas says, ushering them into the house. "I've got some things ready for lunch. You must be starved."

"Mostly tired. And glad to be out of the truck," Sasha says. "It was a long trip. The house is beautiful," she adds.

Michelle says nothing, watching them with her tilted green eyes.

"Well, then, let me just show you where you're going to stay," Dorcas says, too heartily. "I'm putting you in two little rooms on the third floor. I think you'll find them comfortable *and* charming, but you'll have to come down to the second floor to the bathroom in the hall."

"Mom," Sasha says, "you don't have to sell us anything, and you don't have to apologize. Anything at all is going to be fine."

Dorcas leads the way upstairs, letting them peer into the large guest rooms with queen-size beds and the quaintly old-fashioned bathroom. At the end of the hall she opens a narrow door and continues up the steep, enclosed stairway to the attic.

She shows them the room with the spindle bed and the quilt appliquéd with butterflies. "This is my favorite," she says. "The bed was in Lovey's home when she was a child, and then it was in our guest room when I was growing up." She wants to tell them about Caroline Vincent, who once lived in this room, but she decides to wait because Sasha doesn't need more sadness.

In the other room a pair of daybeds fit neatly under the steeply sloping roof on each side of a dormer window. A washstand with a china pitcher and bowl separates them. "And this is for you two."

⚜

Sasha and Michelle are soon in the kitchen, making cottage cheese and apple butter sandwiches. "I tried to find all the things you used to like, Sasha," Dorcas says, "but this is the land of iceberg lettuce and bunny bread."

"It looks great, Mom," Sasha says.

"We're vegetarians," Michelle declares.

"You are?" Dorcas asks, incredulous. She thinks of the pot roast simmering in the Dutch oven. They carry their sandwiches into the dining room. "What do you do about protein?" Dorcas asks.

"Oh, you know—lots of beans, tofu, stuff like that."

Dorcas sighs. "I'm cooking a pot roast to make beef pot-pie. You always loved that."

"Beef potpie!" Sasha crows, suddenly animated. "Real, traditional beef potpie? God, I've been hungry for that." She glances at Michelle. "You've probably never had anything like it. Potpie is a local specialty. It's not even a pie."

"It's not exactly vegetarian," Dorcas says. She's watching Michelle, too, but Michelle's expression gives away nothing.

"Don't worry about it, Mom. As long as I'm in Juniata, I think I'll be a carnivore."

"It'd be better for you to stick to a healthy diet," says Michelle. "With all the stress."

Sasha jumps up, shoving back her chair, and bolts from the room. Michelle follows her, leaving Dorcas sitting alone.

CHAPTER 20

The beef is tender, the onions and potatoes are almost done, and the noodle dough has been rolled out. But Dorcas hesitates. Maybe this was a bad idea.

"What can I do?" Sasha asks. There are deep circles under her eyes.

"You could dish up the cole slaw. And slice the pickled beets and eggs."

What could be better: two women in the kitchen, cooking together. It seems like a natural time to talk, to say things that lie close to the heart. "There's so much I want to say to you," Dorcas says. "How things are in your life. What you're thinking about. I know how devastated you must be about your father. But so much has changed—"

Sasha laughs a little. "Talk about change! Look at you! Everything is different from when I saw you last. Whatever happened to that guy you were going with? Gus? Is he the reason you decided to move back to Juniata, to get away from him?"

"Gus was just part of it. A small part of it." Dorcas has made up her mind to be honest, and she tries to explain how she felt she had to change something. "Seeing this old house seemed prophetic. It was a chance to jump-start my life, steer it in a new direction—if you'll pardon the auto-motive comparisons."

"Did it work?"

"Well, it seems to be working. But, Sasha, I really want to hear about you. Tell me—"

At that moment *goddamned* if Michelle doesn't walk in, and the conversation shuts down as though an engine has suddenly failed. Then the front door opens, and Lavinia yoo-hoos, and Sasha rushes out to greet her grandmother. Michelle trails after her, and Dorcas drops the noodles into the pot.

At dinner, Lavinia says, "Tell me about yourself, Michelle. Where are you from? Who are your parents?"

"Whoa!" Michelle says, passing on the potpie and help-ing herself to pickled beets and eggs. "That's a lot to cover."

"Take your time," Lavinia says, undeterred. "My grand-daughter tells me that you're interested in movies."

"I'm a filmmaker," Michelle says stiffly.

Lavinia leans closer. "And what, exactly, is the difference between making *films* and making *movies*?"

"Artistic sensibility," Michelle replies. "Authenticity. Honesty. Beauty." She passes the bowl to Sasha.

"Ah, you're an artist!" Lavinia cackles and claps her hands delightedly. "Hurray for you! Has my granddaugh-ter told you that I'm an artist? A painter interested in hon-esty and beauty, too. And what was the third one?" She looks to Sasha for help.

"Authenticity," Sasha murmurs. "And yes, I've told her."

"Authenticity, that's it! I'm doing a little writing now, too. On the side." Lavinia's blue eyes are wide. "I'm working on my memoirs." She darts an amused glance at Dorcas, who opens her mouth and closes it again. "I find I have a lot more to say than I expected." She unfolds a napkin and lays it across her lap. "I would find your comments on my paintings very interesting, I'm sure. Now, tell me—are you more interested in the visual aspects of film or the story or *what*?"

"Sasha and I are partners," Michelle explains. "She thinks in terms of story and character. I'm the one who thinks visually."

Dorcas listens in amazement as her mother gets the two women talking openly. But what's this about memoirs? She hasn't heard her mother say Word One about memoirs before this moment.

The dishes have made their rounds. "Potpie always makes me think of Sister," Sasha says. "I feel like I'm digging my way back to my childhood with a knife and fork." Sasha turns to Michelle. "My great-aunt," she explains. "She always called me her little gypsy sweetheart. I was the only one in the family with brown eyes, like a gypsy. Everybody else has the Juniata blues, as she called them, but I was different. Even Dad has blue eyes."

Dorcas jumps up. "You know what I've forgotten? I bought some nice wine—a red zinfandel that should go very well with beef potpie. Mother? Sasha? Michelle? Wine, anybody?" Only Michelle accepts.

Dorcas rushes into the kitchen and wrestles the cork out of the bottle. She pours two glasses—one for herself, one for Michelle—gulps some of hers, refills it, and leans against the kitchen counter. *Little gypsy sweetheart!*

❧

She had thought it would be so easy to get pregnant, but it wasn't. She'd been married for seven years; she was thirty. The doctor kept reassuring her there was nothing wrong. Alex saw no reason to undergo any tests himself, convinced that performance was the key; the demands of his job had taken the edge off, he said. She begged him—he wanted a child as much as she did—but he refused.

She had never had an affair, never even considered it, although she was feeling increasingly distant from Alex. Then one weekend, when Alex was out of town, an opportunity presented itself. She didn't hesitate. Nine months later, Sasha was born. She's never told anyone.

When Sasha was born, Alex fell in love. He spent hours simply gazing at her, as though he could not get enough of this child. His joy helped to cancel out some of Dorcas's guilt.

"Looks exactly like her father," everyone said, "except for those brown eyes."

"Gypsy eyes," said Sister. "My little gypsy sweetheart," she crooned, a song from the 1920s.

For several years after Sasha was born, Alex hoped for a second "miracle baby," but Dorcas knew there would not be another one, short of a different kind of miracle.

❧

"We must have a toast," Lavinia is saying. Seated across from Dorcas at the dining table, she raises her water glass. "To all of us. And that includes you, too, Michelle."

"I'll drink to that." Michelle clinks her glass against Lavinia's. She turns to Sasha, still holding out her glass.

Dorcas notices the tattoo on Michelle's wrist, some kind of a flower. "To our family," Michelle says, "and to its newest member."

Sasha stares, open-mouthed. Dorcas sucks in her breath, waiting for whatever is coming.

"Now what is *that* supposed to mean, Michelle?" Lavinia asks. Her water glass trembles in her hand.

"It means you're going to have a great-grandchild. Sasha's pregnant. Due in November."

Dorcas gapes at Michelle, and then at Sasha, who is studying her plate.

"Well, for goodness sake," Lavinia says and sets down the glass with a thump. "This is certainly news, Sasha. And who may I ask is the father?"

"Coparent," Michelle corrects. "We call it coparenting these days. And the answer is: I am."

"You're *what?*" Lavinia demands, glaring at Michelle. Then she shifts her gaze to Sasha. "Sasha, please explain this. I'm an old woman and a little slow on the trigger."

Sasha picks nervously at her cuticle. She seems close to tears. "Well, Lovey," she says, addressing her thumbnail, "it's about—"

"Love," Michelle interrupts. "It's about me loving Sasha and Sasha loving me. And wanting to have a child together. So—"

"Lesbians," Sasha whispers.

Lesbians? Dorcas spills her wine, blots it quickly, and Lavinia, for once, is completely speechless.

"But the physical *father*," Dorcas interjects, trying to focus on facts. "Who is he?"

"A sperm donor," Michelle explains. "We chose someone whose genetic material seemed compatible with our own."

Suddenly the whole thing strikes Dorcas as hilarious. *Sperm donor!* She bursts out laughing and sprays a mouthful of zinfandel all over her polished table. "You don't even know—" she begins, pounding her fist softly on the table. "Oh, you don't even know!"

CHAPTER 21

Sasha shuts herself up in Dorcas's bedroom after dinner and calls Ellen, her father's wife. When she emerges, weeping, Dorcas moves to put her arms around her, but Michelle beats her to it.

"It's not going to be much longer," Sasha says thickly, leaning into Michelle's embrace. "I told her we'd be there Sunday." She glances at Dorcas. "Is that all right with you?

Dorcas hesitates: *I do not want to do this.* "Sure," she says. "I'll make the arrangements."

Abruptly Lavinia declares that it's time to go home. "I'm fading," she says. A cloak of tiredness seems to have fallen on her, and she droops under its weight.

"Do you want me to drive you?" Dorcas asks.

Lavinia insists that a walk will do her good. Then Sasha says she needs to pick up some things at a drugstore; she doesn't want company either, and Michelle hands over the keys to the truck. "Be careful, babe," she says.

Michelle changes into shorts and a tank top that expose her stringy, freckled arms and legs and announces that she's going for a run.

"There's a nice path that follows the river," Dorcas says. "Take a left at the light. It's about six blocks."

Now Dorcas is alone. She goes upstairs and checks the hall bathroom. It is, as she expects, a mess. The shower curtain has not been tucked inside the claw-footed tub—even though she's posted a discreet notice in a place where she thought it couldn't be missed—and there's a puddle of water on the floor. Rod Benner wanted to put down vinyl flooring here and in the private baths, but she insisted on keeping the original wide pine boards. Now she mops up the water and thumbtacks the notice in a different spot: *Please be sure the shower curtain hangs inside the tub.*

Dorcas climbs to the attic. Sasha and Michelle have evidently decided to change rooms. Jeans and shirt lie crumpled on the antique spindle bed where Lavinia sent Alex to sleep when he came to Juniata for the first time. Dorcas had crept down the hall from her own room and into this same creaking bed, under this same butterfly quilt, and Alex had held her against him. They'd made love slowly, Dorcas biting into the hand Alex pressed over her mouth to silence her moans. Somehow Alex had not been prepared with a rubber, and for the next two weeks Dorcas had worried—unnecessarily, as it turned out. After that, she'd gone to a doctor and been fitted with a diaphragm.

Tracing her fingers over the black stitches that outline the butterfly wings, she thinks of Alex and shudders. It's been a long time since she loved him, but she hates the thought of him suffering. She wonders what he thinks about now. If he ever thinks of her. And if he does, if he thinks of her kindly. If he has finally forgiven her, after all these years.

❧

Even after Sasha was born, Alex worked late most nights, and when he was at home, he shut himself up in the den. He and Dorcas ran out of things to say. They rarely made love.

A year passed, and then another. They'd been married almost twenty years. Things had gotten neither better nor worse. She and Alex didn't argue. They lived separate lives, so there was hardly anything to argue about.

"Listen," Dorcas finally told him, "this isn't working." It was April, rain drumming softly on the windows.

"What?" Alex had looked up from shining his shoes. He had a half dozen pairs lined up in a semicircle on newspapers, and his wooden box that held the little cans of polish—black, brown, cordovan—his rags, his brushes, his buffing cloths.

"Us," she said. "This marriage. I mean, it isn't even a marriage, is it?"

He stared at her for a moment and then went back to applying polish to his black Florsheims.

"So," he said. "What do you propose to do, Dorcas?"

"Quit pretending. Get a divorce. At least a separation."

"And Sasha? What about her? I see that you have thought this through. Figured it all out very carefully." With an old toothbrush he worked polish into the crevice where the upper met the sole.

"No, I haven't." A partial lie: she'd played out similar conversations with Alex in her head a hundred times. "I don't know about Sasha. We can work it out. She stays with me and spends weekends and holidays with you. Alternate holidays. Lawyers decide things like that."

She was shaking, but she felt she was handling it well.

One black oxford gleamed dully in his hand. Alex began to scrub a brush briskly over it, starting at the toe and working back to the heel. He set that shoe down and picked up its mate. "And you have convinced yourself this is what you want."

"Yes. I think so. I mean, I think we should try it. Maybe see a marriage counselor," she added.

"Charlatans," he said scornfully.

She waited for him to say more, waited through all six pairs of shoes. He said nothing. His refusal to respond always made her want to throw things, just to get a reaction. But she'd tried the dramatic approach a few times, and it never worked. He ignored her, shut her out as though she'd ceased to exist. That night they slept in the same bed, facing in opposite directions, careful not to touch. As always.

The next day she came home and found Alex packing. The pants and jackets that hung in neat rows in the closet had been transferred to a bar installed across the backseat of his car. Stacks of shirts from the laundry, piles of folded boxer shorts and tee-shirts, a mound of dark socks rolled into tight balls, handkerchiefs ironed and folded—all this was stuffed into suitcases. The shoes were in shoe bags.

"I have rented an apartment," he said. He smiled, that thin, mirthless smile she detested. "You may communicate with me through my attorney."

"You have a lawyer already?" She hadn't even thought of whom to call.

"It seemed like a good idea, under the circumstances."

"What about Sasha?" she asked. "How should we tell her?" Her voice was trembling; so were her hands.

"Tell her it was your idea, not mine. I have left her a note, saying that I will pick her up after her swim meet on

Saturday morning and bring her back here at five o'clock Sunday afternoon. Please make sure that she has a bag packed to stay overnight. I'll answer her questions then, insofar as I know the answers. And I'll take the rest of the cartons in the den when I drop her off. Unless you have some objection?"

Dorcas had watched from the dining room window as Alex carried two suitcases out to his car and drove away. She stumbled into the den. Several cardboard boxes were stacked in a corner, and most of Alex's things were gone from his old desk, including a picture of Sasha and Alex on skis, wearing matching knitted caps. The framed photograph of the three of them, taken when Sasha was eight, was not on the bookshelf. Dorcas found it in a drawer, facedown.

She called Barbara from the phone on the empty desk and told her Alex had moved out. "I'll pick up a couple of pizzas and bring the twins," Barbara said. "We'll be right over."

By the time Sasha came home from Drama Club, Dorcas had rehearsed her own little speech. She put her hands on Sasha's thin shoulders and explained that Daddy had decided to live someplace else while they worked out some problems. "But there's nothing to worry about, Sasha. Everything will be fine. This has nothing to do with you," she added, because she knew kids often thought a divorce was their fault.

Sasha jerked free and glared at her, cold as marble, exactly the way Alex had glared at her while he polished his shoes. Sasha was twelve, an age at which girls learn to hate their mothers, and Sasha had already mastered this. When she raced upstairs, Dorcas followed her. Sasha read the note Alex had left on her pillow, her face darkening.

"You did this! You!" she shrieked.

Barbara and her twin daughters arrived at the end of the scene. Barbara hugged Sasha, who ducked away, and the girls commandeered the sausage pizza and thundered up to Sasha's room.

Dorcas and Barbara sat at the kitchen table with a bottle of white wine and the anchovy pizza between them. "Okay," Barbara said. "From the beginning. What happened?"

Dorcas was grateful to have Barbara—someone, anyone—there to listen to her story while she tried it out. She couldn't begin to imagine what the next chapter might be.

"You had to do it," Barbara said as they finished off the wine. "I've seen this coming for a long time. You'll be just fine."

She'd been on the brink of finally telling Barbara the rest of the story, a story she'd never told anyone, but then she stopped herself. This wasn't the time. It might never be.

✿

How is it possible? Lavinia appears unfazed by Michelle's revelations. Dorcas finds herself more stunned than her mother, who almost seems to take the news in stride. It occurs to Dorcas that she knows even less about her mother than she does about her daughter. For years she has believed she carried the only secret in the family.

But she's never considered how she'd react if her own daughter turned out to be gay. She still wonders if Lavinia really gets it, actually understands what Michelle was talking about.

Dorcas is rattled by how dangerously close she came to blurting out her own secret. She pours herself a glass of red zin and calls Rootie. "They're here," she says. "Or they were. Sasha drove out to Wal-Mart. And Michelle's out jogging."

"Michelle? That's Sasha's friend?"

"Yes." She doesn't intend to say anything more just now. "It's a long story—I'll tell you when I see you. But here's the thing: Sasha wants to leave Sunday for Connecticut. She talked to Ellen, and it's not sounding good. We'll take off right after brunch. Do you still think you can handle taking over here?"

"I'll give it my best shot," Rootie promises. "How long are you planning to be gone?"

Dorcas doesn't know. It depends—on how bad it is for Alex, on how long Sasha wants to stay. "Tell you what: come over for lunch tomorrow, you can see everybody, and then I'll go over everything with you. A crash course in running a B&B."

She starts making lists. She writes out breakfast menus with recipes, plus a list of groceries she'll have on hand and a second list of items Rootie will need to pick up fresh. Rootie must be here to greet the group making a historical tour and get them settled. That group checks out next Thursday, and the Kruger family isn't due until Friday—ten people staying in the house, two more families parking their RVs in the back. That makes sixteen for breakfast for three days, and she's agreed to provide a picnic buffet for them on Friday evening.

Picnic menu, she writes; *ham, potato salad, baked beans.* Rootie's going to need help with that. Bonnie?

She starts another list. *Call Bonnie. Call Charlie. Call Rod.* Maybe he'll stick around, come back and have dinner with Rootie.

She still hasn't figured out where they'll stay in Connecticut. *Call Barbara.*

The front door opens and bangs shut. "God, I'm tired," Sasha says, and collapses into a rocking chair. "Where's Michelle?

"Out jogging." Dorcas smiles at Sasha, who is rocking, rocking. She looks worn-out. "Are you all right, Sasha?"

"I'm okay. It was a long trip, that's all."

"Your news came as kind of a surprise," Dorcas ventures.

Sasha turns her face away. "I guess it did."

"So, do you want to talk about it?"

"What do you want to talk about?"

This reminds Dorcas of Sasha as a teenager, the with-holding of information, offering only the sketchiest of details, leaving out anything that might alert her mother. Sasha usually didn't lie; she simply omitted large chunks of critical truth, forcing Dorcas to pry, to phone the parents of friends to fill in the blanks.

"Sasha," she says, exasperation breaking through the thin skin of her good intentions, "I don't even know where to begin. I'm surprised that you've decided you're a lesbian. I'm surprised that you're pregnant. I'm surprised that you and Michelle have decided to be coparents, whatever that means. I'm surprised at a lot of things."

"You don't like Michelle, do you?"

"I don't even *know* Michelle. I'm assuming that, if you care for her, she must be a good person."

The front door opens and closes again, and Michelle stands before them, breathing hard. "Hey," she says. She swipes her forearm across her brow. Her sweaty tank top clings to pointy little nipples. Her rat-colored hair sticks up in damp spikes.

"Good run?" Sasha asks. Her eyes soften, a smile erases the fatigue around her mouth.

"Good enough." She turns to Dorcas. "Pretty river. Looks like a nice little town, too." She drops onto the rug, bending one leg at an angle and reaching back in a stretch.

"Juniata has its charms."

"Name three." Michelle stretches the other leg, skewed in what appears to be an impossible position. "Only kidding."

"I've been thinking," Dorcas begins, "that we need to work out a plan. I have to make arrangements to get people to run the show while I'm away. If you still want me to go with you."

But Sasha doesn't have the energy to think about it. "Whatever you decide is fine with me," Sasha says, yawning. "I'm going upstairs. I'm really wiped."

Michelle reaches out and squeezes Sasha's ankle. "Go on, babe. I'll be up soon." Sasha bends down and kisses her. On the mouth. Dorcas looks away.

Dorcas dreaded Sasha's coming-of-age sexually. Barbara used to laugh at her. "I put the twins on the Pill the minute they hit puberty," she said, but that was before AIDS and all the other STDs. When Dorcas herself was an adolescent, she'd thought about sex more or less constantly. When she was newly divorced and past forty, she was embarking on her own explorations at the same time that she worried about Sasha's discovery of sex. What if Sasha came out of her room some morning and stumbled into one of her mother's lovers? All the experts declared it was bad parenting to have illicit sex when a child whose morals were still as impressionable as wet cement lived with you.

Dorcas thinks of Gus, his rush to leave her bed in order to get home to set a good example for his teenage son. Gus was right, no doubt. He was a much better parent than she was—more prudent, more watchful. The proof, as Lavinia

178

would say, is in the pudding: look how Sasha has turned out, a college dropout, married at nineteen, divorced at twenty, a pregnant lesbian at twenty-five.

It's all my fault, Dorcas thinks. *I was a lousy wife and a lousy mother.*

So now she is reaping the results of her ineffectual mothering. Except that Sasha, if you leave out the pregnant-lesbian factor, seems like a genuinely nice person who cares deeply for her lover, her father, her grandmother. Even for her lousy, ineffectual mother.

She wonders what Michelle and Sasha do in bed together. She wonders if it's better than being with a man. A woman would know how to make sure she was satisfied. But how do they work that out? Does one go first, then the other? Do they take turns? And exactly HOW? Fingers, tongues, vibrators?

Sasha has gone upstairs, and Dorcas is alone with Michelle. "Would you care for something to drink?" she asks, like a gracious hostess.

"A beer would be good, if you've got one."

Dorcas gets a beer for Michelle and the last of the zin for herself. Michelle holds the Rolling Rock by the neck and tips it up, swallowing smoothly. She sets the bottle on the floor and wipes her mouth on the back of her hand. "So let's get on with it. You tell me what you need to figure out here."

"Alex could last for weeks."

"Then we'll stay weeks."

"But can you afford—?" Dorcas says, and lets her worry trail off.

"I can always get a temp job. But I think it's important for Sasha to have this opportunity to work things out with her father. Bring some closure."

Jeez, she sounds like a shrink. Like Wellborn. Irritated, Dorcas asks, "Do you have a family, Michelle?"

"Not one I want anything to do with." She grimaces. "I don't set much stock in relatives. What does blood count for, anyway? My idea is intentional families—you choose who you want."

Dorcas nods. *So why did my daughter choose you?*

"It's different for Sasha. She's been talking about you and Lovey since I met her. She's wanted to come east for a visit since long before she knew Alex was sick. She's taking it hard, that he's on his way out. So," Michelle shrugs, "here we are." She pulls her knees to her chin, the empty beer bottle wedged between her feet. "So," she continues, "are you shocked?"

"Shocked?" Dorcas stalls.

"Come on, Dorcas—about Sasha and me. But mainly about Sasha. That she's gay. I take it you didn't know before."

"Not until you outed her, I didn't," Dorcas says coolly. "Is that how you planned it? To save her the trouble of telling me, in the event that I couldn't work it out on my own?"

Michelle sucks the empty bottle for any lingering drops. "I just like things to be clear and open. I don't like secrets. They get in the way. And I have a feeling you have some secrets of your own. I could be wrong, of course."

"No, Michelle, you're entirely right. But they're *mine*, and I'll decide when and how to reveal them. And *if*."

"But you almost did, back there at dinner. You almost let some cat out of the bag. What was it?"

"None of your business, Michelle." Dorcas catches the light in Michelle's tilted eyes. *Nosy little bitch!*

"Whoo-ee! Did I hit a nerve, or what?" Michelle jackknifes and springs to her feet. Dorcas ducks reflexively. "Christ! Now you're afraid I'm going to attack you!"

"No!" Dorcas protests. "Listen, Michelle, sit down a minute, all right? We don't have to like each other, but we do need to get along, at least for the next few days. For Sasha's sake."

⚜

Unable to sleep, Dorcas is up before sunrise Saturday morning, long before the others are awake. She puts on a pot of coffee while she showers, and she's at the kitchen table, dithering over her lists again, when Rod appears at the door. "I'm on my way to a job, and I just wanted to bring you this." He drops a flat metal disc, dangling from a chain, on the table. "My dad got this in high school when he saved a couple of kids from drowning. He wore it all through World War II," he says. "Claimed it brought him luck. So I wore it in the navy, and whenever times get tough, I get it out again. I just thought you might want to borrow it. Times might get tough in Connecticut."

He's gone before she can protest or even thank him properly. Dorcas examines the disc: "For outstanding courage, awarded to Charles Benner, Class of 1931." She drops the medal in her pocket.

Barbara calls while Dorcas is making waffles. "Okay, I've got it figured out. The model apartment in one of Harold's investment properties is available—two bedrooms, furnished, use of the pool and workout room and sauna. You can stay as long as you need it. Gratis."

What would she do without Barbara?

"Actually," Barbara says, "there are two things I need to tell you. The first is that Harold and I are separated—it's friendly, but nevertheless. The second is that Gus is marrying his dentist."

CHAPTER 22

Alex's house is set back from the road in a grove of evergreens. "Here we go," Dorcas says. She can feel Sasha trembling, and her arm tightens around Sasha's shoulders. With her free hand she presses the bell. The door opens, and Ellen's gaunt, worried face appears, her eyes smudged with fatigue and sorrow.

"Oh, sweetie, I'm so glad you're here," Ellen cries, her thin arms clasping Sasha like vines. Ellen and Sasha murmur together tearfully while Dorcas teeters uncertainly on the doorstep, until Ellen seems to remember that someone else is there, too, and leads them inside.

To Dorcas, it's as though Alex's wife and Alex's daughter are a family and she's an outsider. She feels the way she used to, when Alex and Sasha went off skiing or camping together, a twosome that excluded her. You'd have thought, as she watched him years ago with his young daughter, that he'd produced Sasha all by himself without any help from her.

Dorcas swallows a heartburn of jealousy. "How is he?" she asks.

Ellen shakes her head. "It's not good, Dorcas. Sasha, dear, you may not—" She breaks off. "Come on back and say hello to your father, Sasha. He's been waiting for you for so long."

Dorcas hesitates again, unsure what to do. Should she go with them? Or let Sasha visit her father first and then step in later? There are no roadmaps for this trip, no rule books.

Sasha solves her dilemma. "Come on, Mom," she says in a small, pleading voice that sounds as needy as when she was a child. "I want you to come with me." She clutches Dorcas's hand.

"I'm right here, Sasha," Dorcas whispers, trying to project strength around her daughter like a protective shield.

Alex's old study has been turned into a sickroom. The curtains are drawn, and a desk lamp cloaks the room in umber shadow. Alex lies on the hospital bed, his body a shrunken bundle beneath the white coverlet, his emaciated arms extending from the gaping sleeves of a hospital gown. Plastic tubing delivers oxygen to his nose, drips liquid into his veins. He turns his head slightly and stares up, the light in his once lively blue eyes now only a dim flicker in his sunken face.

Dorcas remembers when her own father was dying. Each time she saw him, it was a shock; each time there was less than the time before. Gradually Edgar left his body, his life, all of *them* behind, shucking off everything little by little until there was nothing of her father but her memories.

With an effort Alex reaches toward Sasha. "H'lo," he rasps. "How you?"

Sasha bends down and kisses him and begins to sob quietly. As Alex strokes Sasha's hair, Dorcas sees the thin bones of his hand beneath a nearly translucent web of skin, bruised from needles. She forces herself to step closer and take that fragile hand that once brought her pleasure. He shifts his burned-out gaze from Sasha and settles it on Dorcas. "You—did—right," he says, struggling with each word. The cool hand grips hers, once.

Later, Sasha weeps softly as Dorcas drives her back to the borrowed apartment, where Michelle waits. "It's so hard to see him like that. Why didn't Ellen call me weeks ago? I'd have come sooner, if I'd known," she says.

Dorcas reaches over and squeezes Sasha's knee, thinking of Alex's words. "You did right." *What did he mean?* she wonders. *What did he know, or think he knew?*

⚜

During the night, a call from Ellen awakens them; Alex is in crisis and is not expected to last until morning. They rush back to the house; as Sasha runs into her father's room, Michelle insists on going with her. Dorcas lingers in the hall, her attention caught by a watercolor near the door. She and Alex found it in Martha's Vineyard, a seascape with a wild beach, and they bought it because it reminded them both of Ocean City.

"What a summer that was!" Alex said as he hung the painting in the den of their new house. Dorcas wondered how closely her memories matched his of that one intense week when she met two irresistibly exciting Hungarian boys and ended up marrying one of them. The wrong one.

She's still gazing at the ocean scene when Michelle slips out of Alex's room.

"It's over," Michelle reports in a flat voice.

⚜

Ellen has hurled herself into a frenzy of activity, making phone calls, planning the funeral service with her priest, hiring a caterer to serve lunch afterward. Sasha has shut herself in Ellen's bedroom, supposedly working on her father's obituary, but when Dorcas offers to help, Sasha thanks her but says she needs time alone.

Feeling unneeded and unwanted, Dorcas steps through the French doors onto the flagstone terrace and finds Michelle slumped on a stone bench, staring into a coffee mug. For once, Dorcas feels a bond with Michelle, an outsider like herself. She sits down on the end of the bench.

"So how are you doing?" Michelle asks.

"Okay, I guess. I'm just not sure where I fit in." The chill of the stone seeps through the seat of her pants.

"Same place I do. We're here for Sasha." She scuffs at the mossy flagstones with her sandal.

"You're right." Her butt freezing, Dorcas stands up and wanders through Ellen's English garden. She assumes it's Ellen's—Alex never liked gardening. *Never liked a lot of things, except his goddamned job*, Dorcas thinks bitterly. Unless Sasha wanted to do it, of course. If Sasha had even *hinted* that she wanted a garden, he'd have been up to his ass in alstromeria.

As the morning passes, Dorcas realizes just how superfluous she is. Who is less important at a man's funeral than his ex-wife? Even Michelle has found her role: she's in the kitchen. When Ellen's friends stop by with a casserole or a plate of muffins, Michelle takes care of it. At noon she arranges a buffet in the dining room and coaxes Sasha to eat something, and Ellen, too. Dorcas serves herself fruit salad.

The afternoon drags by slowly. The florist's truck comes and goes, and at last Dorcas is given a job, finding places to put the arrangements when they're delivered. As she sets a vase of miniature roses on the coffee table, she glances at the card stuck on a little plastic trident: "My heart is with you. Fondly, Lavinia."

Unexpected memories blindside Dorcas. On the living room wall she notices the Molnar family coat-of-arms that she worked for Alex in needlepoint the winter before Sasha was born. On the mantel there's a piece of pottery she and Alex picked up in Mexico, along with an intestinal bug. It was their fifth anniversary, she still wasn't pregnant, and Alex blamed *her*, refusing to undergo any tests himself.

Later, she calls Rootie to bring her up-to-date. Rootie offers condolences. "Are you all right, Dorcas?"

"I'm all right, but it's rough on Sasha. I don't think she's eaten a bite since we left Juniata. The funeral isn't until Thursday, but I should be home Friday in time to help out with the Krugers."

"Take as much time as you need. The historical tour people love the place," Rootie reports. "Charlie's a big help, and so is Rod. He has an almost proprietary interest in this place. Or maybe a proprietary interest in *you*?" Rootie lets the question hang; Dorcas lets it go. "Anyway," Rootie continues determinedly, "don't worry about a thing."

※

That evening she decides that a visit to Barbara may be what she needs. Barbara greets her in a slinky black dress with considerable cleavage. She's putting on a final layer of makeup.

"Oh, Dorcas," Barbara says, "I'm sorry, I've got a date tonight. But come on in—he won't be here for another twenty minutes. Tell me how things are going."

"I promise I'll leave when he gets here. I'll go out the backdoor." She describes what she knows of plans for the funeral, at which Ellen's two sons will deliver eulogies. Unwilling to talk about Alex, she steers the conversation in a new direction. "You never did tell me what happened with Harold," she says.

"Well, kiddo," Barbara sighs, "*you* I can tell the truth. I had a fling, a harmless little affair with my tennis pro. But Harold found out. I got careless—maybe in over my head with it, too. I don't know." She tries to smile.

There's no such thing as a harmless affair, Dorcas thinks. *There's always a consequence. Always.*

It seems to Dorcas that Barbara has begun to resemble the aging men they always ridiculed, men with thinning hair and potbellies who chased after and (unless their breath was too vile, their wienie too shriveled) usually married one of those girls who went for Older Men for their money, their power, their sophistication. So what's Barbara looking for with these young guys? Hasn't she turned into exactly what they always loathed?

"I don't know if we'll go through with a divorce or not," Barbara is saying. "I don't even know if I care. Whoever gets Harold now ends up as his nurse."

The doorbell rings. Barbara leaps to her feet. "Ah! There's Ramon."

"Ramon?" Dorcas scrambles for her bag. "Who the hell is Ramon?"

"My Spanish teacher. *Hasta luego*, Dorcas. I'll see you at the funeral. Be sure to call me if you need anything before then."

❧

Sorting through cartons of her father's the day before the funeral, Sasha finds her parents' wedding album, the white silk cover stained with brown splotches. She reacts as though it's akin to the discovery of an ancient royal tomb. Dorcas assumed the album had been lost or thrown out years ago.

Dorcas and Michelle hang over Sasha's shoulder. There's Dorcas in white satin embroidered with pearls, on the arm of Edgar, jaunty in a linen dinner jacket. "Oh, look at you, Mom!" Sasha cries. "I can't believe you went in for lace and a veil. Even a train!"

And there, waiting at the front of the church, is the near-total stranger she is about to marry: Alex, rigid and expressionless, as though he's carved from wood. She wonders what he was thinking. For all the years of their marriage she'd wondered what he was thinking much of the time and never really knew. Waiting with him is his best man, cousin Toby, dark as a gypsy, forehead creased with a frown.

The bride and groom, exchanging vows at the altar. Alex, lifting her veil. (She remembers Toby standing behind him, gazing over his shoulder into her wide-open eyes as Alex kissed her.) The newlyweds dashing down the aisle, Alex now grinning proudly, Dorcas open-mouthed, as though she's gasping for air. There's a sadness in her eyes, too, but Dorcas may be the only one who sees it.

Sasha turns the pages of the album slowly. In the formal poses of the bride and groom and their attendants, cousin Toby is always present. There he is, proposing a toast to the newlyweds. Hovering nearby as they cut the cake. Smiling as they feed each other the first slice.

There is Dorcas, dancing with Edgar, with Alex, and then with Toby. She remembers that Toby's fast turns on the dance floor made her dizzy, and she clung to him to keep from toppling over.

She feels dizzy now as memories of Toby beat down on her mercilessly: The days on the beach, when they first met. Her attraction to him that never disappeared. The weekend he came to Connecticut to visit them.

She and Alex had planned the visit for weeks, but the night before Toby was to arrive, Alex announced that he had to leave Sunday afternoon on a three-day business trip to Detroit. "You can drop Toby at the train when you take me to the airport limo."

But it didn't happen that way. Alex left and Toby stayed.

It was supposed to be just for an hour or so and a chance for her to ask about the woman he'd married. Instead, she asked the questions that had haunted her for years: "Why didn't you come with me into the water that day at the beach? Why did you leave with Becca?"

"Because I always let Alex have what he wanted," Toby said, reaching for her hand, "and Alex wanted *you*."

"And did you want me, too?"

"Of course I did, Dorcas. I wanted you then, and I want you now."

He tilted her head back and kissed her neck, her ears, and finally her mouth. She didn't stop him, and when his hand slipped inside her blouse and searched for her breast, she didn't stop him then, although she told herself she must. When he hesitated, the question in his dark eyes, she reached for him. Soon he was moving inside her, and it was too late to think of anything but the moment. He stayed for three days. Three days she has never forgotten.

When Alex came home from Detroit, tired and complaining of a headache, Dorcas welcomed him dressed in a sheer black nightgown, poured him a scotch, and drew him into bed. A few weeks later the doctor confirmed that she was pregnant. She was thrilled, of course, and Alex declared himself the happiest man in the world.

It was Christmas when they heard again from Toby. He and his wife were expecting a baby early in the summer. Alex and Dorcas replied with their own good news: their miracle child was due in March.

⊱⊰

While Sasha is combing through a box of later photographs, Michelle picks out a snapshot of a young kid. "Who's this?"

"That's Stephen. He's the son of my dad's cousin, Toby. I've told you about Stephen, remember? We're almost the same age." She glances up at Dorcas, who guards her expression. "He calls me every once in a while, did you know that? Ever since his dad was killed in that car wreck in Spain."

"Where is Stephen now?" she asks carefully. Her heart is hammering too loudly.

"Working in Silicon Valley, I think."

"Jesus, you could be twins!" Michelle remarks. "That's incredible!"

"Funny—I never thought about that. Actually, we were pretty close when we were kids."

Michelle drops the snapshot into the box and studies Dorcas with uncommon interest. "You look pale, Dorcas," Michelle says. "Are you okay?"

⊱⊰

After the funeral, Sasha rides back to the house with Ellen, and Michelle somehow ends up with Dorcas. There is no conversation; for several miles Michelle hums a little tune under her breath that gets on Dorcas's nerves. Then,

190

abruptly, Michelle says, "This is just a shot in the dark, Dorcas, but I have a theory. You want to hear it?"

"Sure," says Dorcas, although she does not.

"My theory is that once upon a time you had an affair with your husband's cousin Toby. How'm I doing so far?"

Dorcas says nothing, although she imagines kicking open the car door and shoving the woman out into traffic.

"So you have a little affair, and bingo, there's the baby you and Alex hadn't been able to produce in what? Seven years? Have I got it right?"

Dorcas feels weak, her breathing labored. She refuses to respond.

Michelle presses on. "Assuming I am right, here's my first question: Did Alex ever figure it out? That there was a surrogate father? I'm just curious, that's all."

Alex's last words echo again in her mind: *You did right.*

"See, Dorcas, the way I look at it, it doesn't matter where the sperm comes from; it's who does the raising."

Dorcas doesn't trust herself to speak. Her mouth is dry as dirt. *You did right.*

Michelle leans forward intently. "My next question is, are you going to tell Sasha?"

Dorcas squeezes the steering wheel as she aches to grip Michelle's throat. "I will not tell her, ever. Would I hurt the one I love most, just to ease my conscience?" She takes her eyes off the road and glares fiercely at Michelle. "And you will not tell her, either. Is that clear?"

❧

"You said to call if I need anything. I need to talk."

"Then come right over, Dorcas. I'm here."

Barbara brings out glasses and a pitcher. "It's sangria. I'm crazy over everything Spanish these days." She fills the glasses. "Now, tell me," she orders.

The sangria slips down her throat like silk. Dorcas closes her eyes. "It's about Alex and Sasha," she says. "He's not her biological father. I swore I'd never tell him or anyone, and I haven't. Not even you, and you know practically everything about me. But now her friend, Michelle—and that's a *long* story—seems to have figured it out. And I don't trust her to keep quiet."

Barbara gapes at her. "Alex isn't her father?" she asks incredulously. "You never told him?"

Dorcas shakes her head.

"Surely he must have suspected!"

"I don't know. He may have."

Barbara is still staring. "Are you going to tell me about this? Was it a love affair, a one-night stand, what?"

"Some of both, I guess." She buries her head in her hands and thinks of all the years she spent yearning for Toby, and of their three days together; her grief when she learned of his death; her gratitude for what she had: Sasha.

Sweat trickles under her blouse and she can't breathe. "I'm sorry, but I'm not ready to say any more right now." Abruptly she struggles to her feet and rushes toward the door, groping for the knob. "I'm sorry, Barbara."

Barbara's voice rings out behind her, "Goddammit, Dorcas, wait! There's nothing to be sorry about!"

CHAPTER 23

The women arrive back in Juniata in the midst of chaos. The Kruger clan has taken over Morgan House. Rootie is cleaning up the remains of the picnic supper. Bonnie, in the kitchen, looks shell-shocked. Loud singing and high-pitched laughter erupt from the backyard, where it appears that the Krugers have sloshed past beer and waded into deep booze. Sasha and Michelle grab their bags and race up to the third floor. Dorcas stops long enough to call Lavinia, even though it's on the late side, to let her know they're home. She hopes her mother can't hear the racket.

"The next few days are going to be hectic," she says. "But when things are quieter, we'll have lunch and I'll tell you all about it."

She decides she'd better go out to the backyard and greet the Krugers and try to calm them down, but as she does, she runs into Rod, striding grim-faced toward the house. When he sees her, though, he breaks into a grin. "I told them to put a lid on it, that we've had complaints.

They wanted to know who I thought I was, and I said I'm the general manager and also a deputy sheriff."

Dorcas is aghast. "Is that true? Has somebody complained?"

"Partly true. I'm the one who complained. And I haven't been deputy sheriff for years."

Rootie, looking wrecked, turns down Dorcas's invitation to stick around for a gin and tonic and announces that she's going home. "You're out of limes," Rootie says. "Good night."

Dorcas turns to Rod. "How about you? Do you mind if we're out of limes?"

The Kruger family quiets down. Rod and Dorcas sit on the terrace outside her bedroom with their drinks, and Rod asks how things went. "Rough in some ways, not so bad in others. Maybe it was your good-luck medal that helped. What about here?"

"Quite smoothly. Even with the Krugers." He hesitates. "This could wait until later, but it's been on my mind. It's about Lavinia."

"What's wrong?" Dorcas sets down her glass.

"Basically, I think she's fine, but, you know, her vision is really going. Charlie was in her garage the other day, and he noticed she's getting all kinds of dings and scrapes on her Lincoln. She got all flustered when he asked her what happened. I just thought you ought to know, that's all."

"Thanks, Rod. I'll talk to her. But getting Lavinia to quit driving won't be easy."

"I know. So don't tell her you heard it from me, okay?"

Dorcas swears secrecy. "Listen, as soon as I get rid of this crowd, I want you to come for dinner. We'll eat out here, in Caroline's Garden. I want you to get to know my daughter. Maybe I'll ask Lavinia to come over, too. If she's still speaking to me."

⁂

Dorcas can't sleep. She can't blame it on the Krugers, because they've apparently called it a night and fallen into a stupor. She slips on a robe and steps out onto her terrace. The garden—Caroline's Garden—is brushed with silvery moonlight. The Krugers left it a mess, of course, and she wanders around, inhaling the scent of honeysuckle and collecting trash. She stops, puzzled, at the sound of running water. It takes a few minutes to find the source.

Under the branches of the old maple, surrounded by ferns, is the statue of a young girl, her skirt billowing out behind her; she holds on to her wide-brimmed hat, and in the other arm cradles a pitcher from which a thin stream of water pours into a basin. Where had that come from? Lavinia, maybe?

Near it, mounted on a stake, is a redwood plaque, the incised letters filled with yellow paint:

CAROLINE'S GARDEN
In memory of Caroline Vincent
Oct 4, 1863—Mar 31, 1875

PART IV

LAVINIA

CHAPTER 24

Dorcas has been back for a week, and everything at Morgan House is going full steam. She keeps telling Lavinia they're going to have lunch and a long talk, but so far it hasn't happened. Dorcas is much too busy. Lavinia thinks it would be better for everybody if she *slowed down*.

Angling her Lincoln into a space across from Morgan House, Lavinia spots the red truck, right smack in front of the entrance. Somebody ought to tell Michelle to park it around in back. Who wants to see an ugly truck in front of a bed-and-breakfast? What kind of advertisement is that?

These Sunday brunches have caught on, even though questions could be asked about certain menu items. That California quiche, for instance, with the artichoke hearts and avocado, did not sit too well on Lavinia's stomach. Stick to the tried-and-true, she's told Dorcas—sausage casserole, pecan waffles—that's the best plan.

Even though it's raining cats and dogs, there's a full house today, but Marge Kramer has saved her a place. Strawberry shortcake is on the menu, and that's tempting. But there's something unpleasant going on—every now and then she hears Sasha and Michelle arguing in the kitchen. If *she* can hear them, so can other customers. Fortunately, Marge is a little deaf. But where on earth is Dorcas?

Lavinia visits some of the other tables, greeting friends, and eventually makes her way toward the kitchen. "Where's the boss?" she asks cheerily. Sasha mutters, "She's around somewhere," but keeps her face averted.

Lavinia lowers herself onto a kitchen chair. She smiles at Michelle and compliments her on the shortcake. The two girls bustle around her. Bonnie, who now wears pants when she's serving, brings Lavinia a cup of coffee without even being asked. She stays put. Finally, Michelle says angrily, "I need to get something out of the truck," and stomps out.

Lavinia waits until she hears the front door close and Bonnie has gone to take out the trash. Then she says to her granddaughter, "Sasha, sweetheart, tell me about all this." She waves her hand toward the front door to indicate the departed Michelle.

"Like what?"

"Like you and Michelle and what's going on."

"We're partners," Sasha says, and Lavinia merely nods. Sasha draws a long, wobbly breath. "And we're having a baby."

"I'm sure you've thought this through carefully," Lavinia says, although obviously they haven't.

"Oh, wow, did we ever!" But before she can say more, a bell jingles, a signal that the front door has opened.

"Come see me, Sasha," Lavinia whispers. Aloud she says, "Well, I can't imagine what's become of that mother of yours." Lavinia rises slowly and prepares a smile for Michelle, whose face is hardened in a frown. "Michelle," she says in her most persuasive manner, "don't you think in the future it might be better to park your truck around in back?"

⸎

Late in the afternoon Lavinia fixes herself a cup of tea and sits at her dining table by the bay window. She has a window open so that she can listen to the rain falling in slow, heavy drops. And her notebook is open to the last entry.

Lavinia hasn't written much in the notebook since she heard about Alex. Poor man; he must have been close to the same age Edgar was when he took sick. Cancer, what a terrible thing.

Lavinia often wonders what it will be that finally carries her off. She isn't being morbid, as Violet Worley insisted when Lavinia introduced the subject at their last bridge luncheon. "Do you think much about dying?" Lavinia asked, and the others laughed nervously and rolled their eyes, except for Violet.

"It's morbid to talk about such things, because there's nothing you can do about it anyway!" Violet cried angrily. "As long as you see your doctor and take your pills and make sure you have a living will, then you might as well squeeze in what pleasure you can, and, as far as I can see, there's damn little at that."

Then Esther Bowersox said she thought death must be a beautiful thing. "I've been reading about after-death experiences, and everybody who came back reported that it was just blissful. Death, that is—not coming back."

Marge Kramer said she thought her John Robert was watching over her from some vantage point in heaven. Lavinia said she hoped *not*. "It would be like being spied on. I wouldn't have wanted to be watched when Edgar was around, and I surely don't want it now." She didn't tell them that she doesn't believe in heaven anyway, no matter what Reverend Burkholder has to say.

⚜

Lavinia lays aside her pen and notebook and rubs her eyes. The hole in the vision in her right eye is getting worse, as the doctor said it would when she saw him in February. So far it's mostly a nuisance, except for driving. She hasn't told Dorcas yet. Or mentioned the dent in her right rear fender, acquired somehow in the church parking lot. But Sasha noticed right away that something was wrong. "Are you having trouble with your eyes?" she'd asked.

"It seems so," Lavinia said. "The doctor says nothing can be done about it. But I'd rather you not mention it to your mother, if you don't mind." She knows that the minute Dorcas finds out, she'll want her to quit driving. She expects quite a scene.

"Don't worry," Sasha reassured her. "I'll keep your secret."

Apparently Sasha's been keeping a few of her own. From the minute Lavinia walked through the front door of Morgan House the day her granddaughter and Michelle arrived from California, she detected something strange going on, starting with Sasha's friend Michelle—hair standing on end and unhappy eyes. So Lavinia kept her own eyes and ears open and her mouth shut, and it all came out, right there at their first dinner.

Being queer seems to be all the rage now. Once upon a time, men and women with such leanings kept it a secret. Michelle is a queer, which is her business and her choice; harder for Lavinia to accept is the notion that this means Michelle and Sasha are not just "friends" but lovers. So Sasha is a queer, too. That sticks in Lavinia's craw. She doesn't buy the theory that people are "born" that way. More than likely Michelle took advantage of some weakness of Sasha's, perhaps her innocence, her need for affection, and seduced her. Not only that, but Sasha is pregnant in the bargain, although God only knows how they accomplished that. Coparenting indeed! Good Lord!

Lavinia watches *Oprah* and *Larry King* and reads the *Philadelphia Inquirer* and *Time,* and she has gotten accustomed to the idea that there are homosexuals living openly in the world. She has even known one personally—her art teacher, Morris Cleveland. She likes to think that she is broad-minded, and she believes such people have as much right as anyone else to live their lives as they wish—Reverend Burkholder be damned.

That does *not* mean that Michelle and Sasha are entitled to bring an innocent child into the picture. Lavinia decides that she'll have to talk to Sasha again.

The presence of Michelle is disturbing for another reason: it has started Lavinia thinking once more about Morris Cleveland. This is the one chapter in her memoirs that may well turn out to be the hardest to write: what to leave in, what to leave out.

She begins: *I owe everything to Morris Cleveland.*

❧

For years, Lavinia did what was expected of women of her generation: belonged to the Music Study Club, volunteered for the Red Cross, kept a nice home for Edgar and Dorcas. She never thought about whether or not it was "fulfilling," as they say now. When Edgar died and she took over Juniata Marble and Granite, she threw herself into the business with gusto she didn't know she had. She'd argued with Edgar that she didn't want it, couldn't do it, but he'd insisted: *Yes you can, Lovey. Yes you can.*

Well, she could; she proved that. She'd run the damned place, with all its labor problems and financial ups and downs, until she was seventy.

When Lavinia was in her sixties, young Morris Cleveland came to town and bought a florist shop. He had such a knack with flower arrangements that from the outset people began to call him with special requests. If you were having a wedding, you'd call Morris. If you wanted a centerpiece for a luncheon, you'd call Morris. He had ideas for gardens, too; Lavinia remembers when he suggested to Marge Kramer that she create a rock garden along the curving walk leading to her front door.

Morris began hanging his watercolors in his shop, paintings of flowers, still lifes with fruit, and his customers began buying them. One day when Lavinia went into the shop to pick up a pot of African violets for Violet's birthday—she did this every year, and it had gotten to be a joke because the plant never survived for more than a couple of months—she noticed an advertisement for painting classes.

"I've never done this before," Lavinia warned Morris when she signed up. "I'm not sure I have any talent."

"Everybody has at least a little," he told her. "Just do it for fun."

I wish he were still around, Lavinia thinks now. *I'll bet he could do wonders for Sasha. And maybe for that sour Michelle, too.*

Six people showed up for the first class; Lavinia knew four of them. Morris introduced them to sketching with charcoal on newsprint, showed them how to use the edge and the flat of the stick, how to smudge and blend, how to use white space. He arranged a milk jug, an egg, an old pillow that drooped limply over the edge of the table, and told them to draw it. He added a single spiky flower to the jug, a patterned cover on the pillow, more eggs. Lavinia, self-conscious, stingy with the use of the large sheet of newsprint, had trouble at first. The next week, Morris put on a record—Gershwin's *Rhapsody in Blue*—and Lavinia found herself released by the jazzy rhythm, as though a cage door had opened and she was free to go wherever she wanted. Evenings, after she had finished at Juniata Marble and Granite, she went home and sketched whatever caught her eye.

She loved Morris. Everyone did. Handsome, buttery Morris with tousled brown hair, dazzling white smile, unforgettable hazel eyes. There was speculation about his age; Lavinia guessed late thirties.

A year of art classes extended to two. As long as Morris offered the course, she signed up for it. Other students joined, stayed for a while, dropped out; Lavinia kept on. She was into color now, and landscapes. Two of her paintings sold at a student show.

She and Morris became close friends, and he began stopping by for a drink once or twice a week. Once Morris suggested going out for dinner, but there was no way in the world she was going to give local gossips something to talk about by showing up with a man at a restaurant in Juniata. Coey, for instance, would immediately decide there was something romantic going on. Instead, she asked him to drive her over the mountains to State College.

At dinner she asked if he had ever been married, and he replied pleasantly, no, he was a bachelor. "Too bad," she said. "There are lots of nice women here in Juniata who'd love to change your mind." He smiled, and she didn't suspect a thing.

❧

When the phone rings later in the week, Lavinia is tempted not to answer. Dorcas gave her an answering machine for Christmas and taught her to screen her calls, and now she waits to find out who it is. But when she hears Sasha's voice, she picks up the receiver.

"Lovey, is it okay if I come over? I need to talk to somebody."

Lavinia is delighted. While she waits for Sasha, she puts the kettle on and sets out two cups, pleased that she has herbal tea to offer. She has a fair notion of what this talk is going to be about: Michelle. Michelle seems to be all rough edges.

The night before they left for Connecticut to visit Alex, Lavinia had invited them to Rocco's for dinner. She'd forgotten Michelle's dietary preferences.

"Not exactly a place for vegetarians," Michelle grumbled, looking over Rocco's menu. Every item on it involved meat.

"Ma'am?" the waitress whimpered when Michelle asked for pesto.

So Michelle ordered spaghetti with olive oil, period, and the waitress was sent back out by the cook to make sure she understood it right. "Obviously you all haven't been coming here for the last half century for the food," Michelle said, passing on the box of grated parmesan.

"Why, Michelle," Lavinia crooned, waving her hands to encompass the drooping fake ivy and the tarnished tarpon above the bar, "it's the atmosphere!"

Later, she proposed giving Michelle a historical tour of Juniata. Dorcas drove while Lavinia supplied commentary on the site of her family's farm, the schools Dorcas and

Lavinia had attended, the house on Lindbergh Way, the monument store.

"You might want to think about making a movie—excuse me, a *film*—in Juniata," Lavinia said, craning around in her seat. "I could tell you lots of stories."

"I'll bet you could," Michelle agreed, and Lavinia wondered if Michelle was mocking her.

Then, as a finale, Dorcas insisted on taking them to the cemetery and showing them the ancient tombstone of a little girl who used to be a servant for William Morgan and lived in the attic room. "The slave quarters," Michelle has been calling it since.

The kettle begins to whistle just as Sasha arrives. When they're settled by the window with their tea, Lavinia grasps Sasha's hand. It's cold, she notices, and trembling. "Now," she says, "tell me what's bothering you."

"Well," Sasha begins, "it has to do with Michelle. See, I've known for quite a while that I'm gay; I figured that out while I was still married. A couple years ago I met Michelle. We were both interested in a lot of the same things—"

"Film," Lavinia says encouragingly.

"Yeah. And then we fell in love." Sasha looks up at her with her great brown eyes. "You remember what that's like, I'm sure." Lavinia nods, although she really can't imagine what it's like to fall in love with a *woman*. "And after we'd been together for a while, we decided that we wanted a child. Michelle has some medical problems in her family, and so we thought I should be the one to have the baby. But I have a better-paying job—managing a restaurant? So after the baby's born, I'm supposed to go back to work, and Michelle will stay at home with him." She grins at Lavinia. "It's a boy. We had the test."

Lavinia smiles back. "It will be nice to have a great-grand-son." But she's thinking, *how do they plan to bring him up, these two gay women?*

"The thing is, I think sometimes I'd be the better one to stay at home, you know? Like, I'm more temperamentally suited. And I just found out that my dad left me some money in a trust—did Mom tell you? Actually, kind of a lot of money—the lawyer says about thirty-five grand a year. So now I can afford to stay home with the baby if I want to, which I do, but Michelle is upset. She wants to be the primary child rearer. The main mom."

"I *see*," Lavinia says carefully. No, Dorcas did *not* tell her about any inheritance! "Well, this does change the picture. I imagine Michelle is worried that the baby will grow up more attached to you, if you're around more."

Sasha looks at her gratefully. "Right. Plus, things won't be equal anymore. Before, neither one of us had any money. Now I do. Everything could be different."

Lavinia thinks over what she wants to say next. "But you and Michelle care about each other."

"Well," Sasha admits, "I'm not sure now about Michelle. We've been fighting a lot lately. Not fighting, exactly, but arguing about stuff. Not even important stuff. She's talking about leaving. She wants us to go back to California."

"And you? How do *you* feel, Sasha?"

"I don't know *how* I feel," Sasha wails. "Sometimes I want to go with her, but I don't know if it's going to work. And sometimes I want to stay here—Mom could use some help at Morgan House—but I don't know if that would work either. My mother isn't the easiest person." She stares into her teacup. "What would you do, Lovey?"

"I'm not sure what I'd do," Lavinia says thoughtfully. "But I think it's important for you and Michelle to work things out. Love is never perfect, after all, and she *is* the co-parent of your child, for goodness sake! Do you think we might persuade her to stay here? She might come to love Juniata."

CHAPTER 25

She opens her notebook and rereads the last page. She's been writing about Morris Cleveland, and it hasn't been easy.

After she retired, she was free to do exactly as she pleased. Trips to State College with Morris got to be a regular event. One September evening as they were coming back from dinner, Morris said, "Let's go to the shore. I grew up in Philly, but can you believe I've never been to Ocean City?"

They went off without a word to anyone on a golden day at the beginning of October. The old Prince of Wales was still in business, but it looked so run-down that Lavinia decided to stay at a new motel at the upper end of the boardwalk.

The tide was out. A ship moved slowly, slowly along the horizon. Lavinia took off her shoes and walked on the sand in her stocking feet, close to the frill of foamy sea-water. Morris rolled up the cuffs of his trousers. A small wave raced in and quickly raced out again, leaving behind a silvery flicker, a fish arching and wriggling, willing itself back to the sea. Morris scooped it up and tossed it onto the next wave.

The next day they went out early and sketched the boardwalk, the bridge, and, later, the fishing boats coming in. They carried their sketchbooks and folding stools to the deserted beach. Lavinia marveled at the speed and deftness with which Morris sketched. By comparison her own work was slow, plodding.

That night, Lavinia wrapped herself in a blanket and sat on her balcony, her slippered feet propped on the railing. She wondered if Morris was in his room watching television. Maybe he'd step out on his balcony to look at the moon on the water, and she'd call out to him and suggest that he come over and join her. She tried not to think of her naked flesh, sagging breasts and slack belly.

Lavinia stops writing. *Of course* he hadn't rushed over and made love to her. She was so caught up in her fantasies about Morris that she never stopped to *notice*. How naive she was, a seventy-year-old innocent, as innocent as she'd been with Nicholas. At that time, she'd imagined it was the age difference.

Her training as an artist continued. Morris started her on figure drawing, using wooden models and photographs in books. Years sped by so quickly she scarcely noticed. Dorcas often referred to Morris as "your chauffeur" or "your escort," aware that they went on trips together. She once said, "You trust this man, Mother? You don't think he's out to take advantage of you?" Lavinia kept mum about the fact that she paid for both of them.

When Lavinia was seventy-five, Morris was pushing fifty—still handsome, although his hair was thinning and he had grown a beard that showed a startling amount of gray. By then Lavinia understood that he was queer, an understanding that had come upon her gradually, and without surprise. He was her friend and her mentor, and she cherished him.

One day he said, "I can't teach you any more, Lavinia. You have the technique, you have the skill. But you're only scratching the surface of what you can do. There's a lot in here that hasn't been touched yet." He tapped his chest. They were having dinner in Lavinia's apartment; Lavinia had supplied the ingredients, and they were drinking Manhattans while Morris cooked, a new arrangement. "I don't wish to be indelicate," he said, mashing a clove of garlic with the flat of a knife, "but you're not getting any younger. If you're going to do some serious work, you'd better get on with it."

She'd been mildly offended. What could he possibly mean? She was selling her landscapes. People loved her Amish paintings—what was wrong with that?

"Nothing is wrong with it," he told her, splashing vermouth on chicken breasts. "But there's no passion." He turned his hazel eyes upon her. He was no longer the handsome younger man she remembered, his thinness seemed haggard, but his eyes hadn't changed. "It's in there somewhere," he said. "Find it, and then paint it."

That was when she finally began to paint Nicholas. It was as though Nicholas had been preserved intact for well over half a century, until her love for Morris released him. Nicholas and Morris fused in her memory.

Shyly at first, embarrassed at herself, at the details she remembered, she began. These would be secret paintings; she'd keep them locked away, hidden even from Morris. At first there were only sketches, rough studies, ideas still to be worked out. She was intrigued by the human body, both fascinated and repulsed by the way it aged and changed. She stood naked in front of her mirror and drew what she saw.

Morris told her about his illness, first making her promise that she would not discuss it with anyone. He had always seemed physically frail; for as long as she'd known him he'd suffered from weak lungs, a hacking cough that lasted from winter until early summer.

She watched helplessly as he shrank down to skin and bone, just as she'd watched Edgar. Sometimes she wished he would hurry up and die and let her grieve in peace.

"I'm moving back to Philadelphia," he told her on the phone one day when she'd not heard from him in a while. "I have a sister there."

Lavinia packed up some of the drawings and paintings that she'd done since she'd let Nicholas back into her head. Then she called Rod Benner and asked him for a favor. She'd pay him for his time, but the favor was that he tell no one. Rod put the paintings in the trunk of Lavinia's car. They drove to Morris's place. A man she didn't know sat in a chair by the bed; when she came, he got up and left.

She was shocked by Morris's appearance, although she had seen him only two or three weeks earlier. The biggest change was in his eyes; they'd flattened somehow, as though a light had gone out. He gazed at her weakly. "I'm tired," he said.

"I know. But I wanted you to see these." Rod brought in the paintings and propped them, one at a time, on a chair next to the bed. The first one was the painting of Nicholas and herself.

He managed a smile. She showed him the next one, Nicholas, alone, beckoning. "I would have loved him too,"

Morris whispered and turned his face away.

⚜

I owe everything to Morris Cleveland.

Lavinia makes a decision. She will show Dorcas the paintings. She will explain about Nicholas. She will explain that she has had secrets. And she will tell her that she is going blind.

PART V

DORCAS AND LAVINIA

CHAPTER 26

It's stopped raining, thank God, predictions are for fair weather—although you never know—and the Larber wedding will take place tomorrow afternoon in Caroline's Garden. Everything is blooming madly: tubs of geraniums, baskets of petunias, peony bushes with their fat, frilly blossoms, roses beginning to swarm over the old-fashioned trellis where the minister will stand; only the pachysandra beds still look a little anemic. In the morning the florist will fill in some of the thin spots with baskets of daisies and ivy, Charlie will come to set up chairs for fifty guests, and at noon the caterer from State College will take over Dorcas's kitchen.

During the hectic weeks since Dorcas has been back from Connecticut, she's not had much chance to talk to Rootie—it almost seems as though Rootie has been avoiding her—and so she's invited Rootie to come over and help wrap silverware. While the wedding party is at a rehearsal dinner at the country club, Dorcas and Rootie sit on the terrace, bundling fifty forks and spoons in blue napkins and tying each set with white ribbon and a packet of forget-me-not seeds. Dorcas has finished telling Rootie most of what went on in Connecticut, filling her in on the situation with Sasha and Michelle, omitting any mention of Toby. Now she wants a report on Rootie's week, to learn if she's made any progress in her campaign to win Rod.

But Rootie is in a rotten mood and seems to be only half listening. Dorcas assumes it's the job at the library and Dirty Don Dixon, the asshole boss, that have turned her friend sullen and pouty. When Dorcas asks as casually as possible, "So how did it go with Rod?" Rootie replies flintily, "He came here every day while you were gone. He even stayed for dinner once. And all he could talk about was *you*."

Dorcas's hand hovers over a fresh stack of napkins. "Me?"

"The man is crazy about you. He said as much."

"Rootie, I had no idea. I didn't!" Dorcas protests, although, truly, she *did* have some inkling that Rod's concern about her might reach beyond friendship. That near-kiss at Christmas comes to mind. But so far, she's managed to ignore it.

"He said, quote, 'I want to get close to her, but I don't think she'll let me,' unquote."

"But that doesn't mean—"

"Dorcas," Rootie cuts in impatiently, "it couldn't be more obvious if he carved 'Rod loves Dorcas' on that tree." She stabs a fork at the ancient oak under which they're sitting.

Now what? Dorcas thinks wearily after Rootie leaves when the last bit of ribbon has been tied, abruptly refusing Dorcas's offer of a gin and tonic. Dorcas mixes one for herself, adding an extra half shot of gin and two chunks of lime, and carries her drink out to Caroline's Garden. She's running on sheer willpower. Every guest room in Morgan House is booked for every weekend from the end of June through Labor Day, plus the whole week of the Fourth of July and the second week in September when the annual bean soup festival will be held at the county fairgrounds. The tension between Sasha and Michelle is as thick as the breakfast oatmeal.

And now this: her two best friends in Juniata—Rod and Rootie—are behaving in ways she hadn't anticipated. She doesn't need this complication. It changes everything! Why couldn't things just stay the way they've been? There's still so much work to be done—converting the former stables to a summer house, for instance. After all this time of having Rod around for one reason or another, all those after-work beers, she's certain now to be awkwardly self-conscious in his presence. And no matter how she handles it, Rootie's bound to feel jealous of the time Dorcas and Rod spend together. As *friends*, goddammit! But Rootie will never buy that, never believe that Dorcas hasn't been interested in him all along.

If she'd been paying attention, she would have noticed before that things had changed with Rod. She should have caught on when she discovered the statue of the young girl in the garden, and Rod refused to take any payment for it. He brushed off the gift: "I found it when I was cleaning out the barn at an old house I'm working on. The owners didn't want it. I thought of you, and of Caroline Vincent." The plaque with Caroline's name and dates? "I had some scrap lumber. It just seemed like a good idea. You don't have to keep it if you don't like it."

She sits on a bench near the statue, listening to the water splashing into the basin at the girl's feet, and sucks on a chunk of lime. *Of course* she likes it. Loves it, in fact.

The good-luck medal he loaned her—that should certainly have tipped her off to his feelings. The medal is still in her drawer, she thinks guiltily, and she still hasn't invited him for the dinner she promised.

Dorcas squints up at the attic and notices the lights on in both bedrooms. It seems that either Sasha or Michelle has moved out of the room with the double bed and into the room with two singles. She has no idea exactly what's going on between them, although she senses that their relationship is not getting better. And there's not a thing she can do to help.

Headlights sweep into the parking area. The wedding party is back from the rehearsal dinner, and Dorcas, mustering up her professional innkeeper's smile, rises to greet them.

❧

The bride, wildflowers woven in her dark hair, walks hand in hand with her groom to the rose-covered trellis, accompanied by the soulful music of a flute. Dorcas, watching with the caterer through the kitchen window, can't help imagining what a beautiful bride Sasha would make, flowers in her hair, but quickly banishes that notion. Sasha, looking pinched and tired, begins pouring the champagne they'll serve when the ceremony ends.

There's no sign of Michelle. Sasha volunteers, "Michelle went for a run. She hates weddings. She says she'll be back to help clean up."

Dorcas doesn't notice Rod, dressed in a suit and tie, until she and Sasha are moving among the guests with a tray of champagne glasses. He smiles at her, acknowledging her unasked question. "The groom used to work for me."

Out of the corner of her eye Dorcas spots Rootie and ducks away from Rod. Rootie manages to corner her. "I acted like a dumb teenager last night. I'm sorry, Dorcas. Do you need any help?"

Dorcas sighs with relief. "It's okay. Just keep an eye on Sasha, will you? We'll catch up later."

❧

It's no surprise to Dorcas when Michelle slings her duffel into her truck and heads for California a day after the wedding. Now that her lover is really, finally gone, Sasha moves listlessly through her days, as though she's not fully awake. She still announces each morning how many days it has been since her father died, and she and Michelle talk on the phone nearly every night, long, secretive conversations. Her pregnancy is beginning to show. Dorcas was relieved at first to have Michelle out of the picture and the arguments done with, but Sasha seems so sad and lonely that Dorcas has come to believe the separation is a mistake. But she has no advice to offer Sasha, except to comfort her.

Sasha is not Dorcas's only worry. It's been a month since Rod spoke to her about Lavinia's eyesight, but Dorcas still hasn't brought it up with her, even when Lavinia casually mentioned some damage to her garage door.

Before the situations get worse, she's got to sit down with her mother and her daughter. She's got to persuade them to talk about how they feel about the losses in their lives, but she can't summon the energy. *As soon as I get through the Fourth,* she promises herself.

❧

The holiday weekend crowd has cleared out, and Dorcas and Sasha are alone in the kitchen. "Mom, listen," Sasha says carefully. "I need to go back to Santa Cruz for a while."

Dorcas has been expecting this. "To Michelle?"

Sasha's knife zips through a bunch of scallions. "I don't know if I'll be going back to Michelle. But I have a job there, and all my stuff." She tosses little circles of green onion into the salad bowl. "I miss her, you know? But I also know it could be a big mistake."

"It could be," Dorcas agrees. "I know I've wasted chunks of my life yearning for the wrong lover, or trying to make something work that was doomed from the beginning. But it could also be exactly the right thing to do, and you probably can't figure that out from here. Besides, you have somebody else to think of now."

Smiling as though she's just been handed a flower, Sasha takes her mother's hand and places it on her growing belly. She holds it there until Dorcas feels her grandchild's first tentative stirrings.

⚜

Dorcas invites Lavinia to ride with them to the airport. Sasha's flight is at one o'clock, and if Dorcas leaves the breakfast cleanup to Bonnie, they can manage it. "I was thinking we might take your car," Dorcas says to her mother. "And you and I can stop somewhere for lunch on the way back."

But Lavinia hesitates. "Oh, Dorcas, I really don't think I'm up to it just now."

Not up to it? Dorcas can't remember ever hearing her mother say that. *Maybe,* she thinks, *Lavinia doesn't want me to see the damaged fenders.*

⚜

Lavinia pours herself a splash of Jack Daniels on the rocks and waits for Dorcas to come back and tell her about her trip to the Harrisburg airport. She didn't go with them because she knew she'd get teary and make a public spectacle of herself; who knows if she'll ever see Sasha again?

She has spent part of the afternoon pulling her paintings out of the hidden closet and hanging them around the walls of her living room, replacing the landscapes and still lifes. She has the notebooks, now mostly filled, and the elegant blank book, still completely empty, arranged on the coffee table. She has rested her eyes, and now she's ready. It's time.

She's decided to turn her notebooks over to Dorcas. The memoirs are finished; she's said all she has to say about her life, although once in a while she wakes up in the middle of the night and thinks of something she wants to add. She's always sure she'll remember it exactly in the morning. Only she doesn't.

She has not, as she planned, copied a single word into the book her friends gave her for her birthday. Nor has she done any revising in the notebooks. It's all become too difficult.

The eye doctor warned her to expect this, but she still has no idea how she'll deal with her eye trouble. He had her fitted with a contraption like a diver's mask with lenses that magnify everything enormously. She puts on the clumsy thing when she paints, but that blank spot right in the middle of whatever she's looking at is unbearably distracting. She paints by peeking sidelong at the canvas. She doesn't have a good eye now; just a bad one and one that's less bad.

Writing in the notebook is even harder than painting. She can't manage to go back through everything, line by line, crossing out and adding to and then putting it all together in the blank book, the way she'd planned. So she's arrived at a compromise: she'll give the notebooks to Dorcas and ask her to copy the *appropriate* parts into the nice book. Dorcas's handwriting isn't as graceful as Lavinia could wish, but it's legible. Sasha will be able to read it.

She freshens her drink and waits.

Dorcas sucks in her breath when she sees Nicholas—beautiful, naked Nicholas, whoever he was—hanging on Lavinia's wall. She'd seen it and the other erotic paintings in Lavinia's closet, but still it's a shock to see the genitals and breasts publicly displayed, hung where there used to be bowls of peaches, vases of iris. Bright daylight illuminates the paintings, giving depth to even the smallest details. The flecks of gold in Nicholas's brown eyes, for instance.

"These are my secrets," Lavinia says. "I thought it was time to show you. To explain. Just go ahead and look, if you want to."

The handsome young man is somehow both earthy and ethereal. But what seizes Dorcas's attention is Lavinia's interpretation of herself, as her beauty matured and altered with age. How honest and strong of her mother to see herself—and to portray herself—so objectively.

She moves from one painting to the next, from the male nudes to the females, aware that Lavinia is watching her for a reaction. She has to remember that her mother doesn't know she's seen them before. In this light, they're even more dramatic than when she'd crept into the closet and looked at them in secret.

"Mother, they're absolutely splendid! I'm very proud of you, and I'm glad that you've decided to show them to me."

"Thank you," says Lavinia. "But aren't you curious? About who he is? How he fits into my life?" She cocks her head to one side, a habit now. Before Dorcas can reply, Lavinia hurries on. "I think it would be better if you just read these notebooks. I planned to write down whatever came to mind, and then take out the parts that seemed unsuitable. I wanted to copy them in final form and to pass that on to you and Sasha. But I can't do it." She sips a little of her Jack Daniels. "I don't see as well as I used to."

This is the opening Dorcas has been waiting for, to bring up the matter of Lavinia's eyesight, and she rushes ahead. "I've been meaning to talk to you about this, Mother. Your vision. I'm a little concerned about your driving."

"A *little* concerned? Huh," Lavinia snorts. "I suppose Sasha's been talking to you. A person can't get a tiny dent in a fender without the whole town knowing it. Well, you can put your mind at ease about that. It's all been taken care of."

"It has? What do you mean?"

Lavinia's chin tilts up at a defiant angle. "I mean I won't be driving anymore. I sold my car to Wanda at the Trolley Stop."

"*Wanda* has the Lincoln now?"

"She offered me a good price, and I accepted it. I can take a lot of taxis for what she paid."

Lavinia, the problem solver. "What about your vision, though?" Dorcas persists. "Have you seen a specialist? Not just the optometrist?"

"Of course I have! And a very good one, too. But the news isn't so good. He called it macular degeneration and claims I'm losing my sight."

"My God, Mother, why haven't you told me before? I knew you were having trouble with your eyes, but I had no idea—" Dorcas reaches out to embrace her mother, but Lavinia has never been much for hugs.

"Goodness, Dorcas," she says sourly, "there's no cause to get upset about this. When you reach my age, you learn to take some of these failings in stride. I'm just thankful I still have all my marbles." She taps her head. "Not like some people."

"But what does the doctor *say*? Is there anything that can be done to stop it? Keep it from getting worse?"

"Apparently not. He did give me this doodad. It helps some." She shows Dorcas a sort of magnifying glasses. "But it's just too hard now for me to read my own writing. Also, there are still some paintings I want to do. I'll save my eyes and my energy for that." She places the pile of notebooks in Dorcas's lap. "Take them home and read them. You'll find out all about Nicholas."

"What about the paintings, Mother?" Dorcas asks as she's preparing to leave; she has guests checking in at five. "Shall I help you put them away?"

Lavinia waves her off. "No, thank you," she says crisply. "I intend to leave them up. I want to look at them while I can still see. When the girls come next time for bridge, it'll give them something to cackle over." She stops suddenly, looking stricken. "Oh, Dorcas, I just thought of something! What will I do when I can't see the cards anymore?" Then she recovers and shrugs. "I suppose I can always enjoy the martinis!"

<hr/>

Dorcas begins reading the notebooks while she drinks tea at her kitchen table. Her mother's life soon distracts her from the absence of Sasha.

I was born on August 22, 1910, the youngest daughter of Clarence and Edna Yingley Miller, in the town of Juniata, named for the river on whose banks it stands . . .

She stays up very late, engrossed, adrenalin rushing. The next morning she serves breakfast to her guests and the regulars and then goes back to the notebooks. She sees everything now through Lavinia's eyes: Nicholas. Lavinia's father. Sister. Edgar. Her own birth. Later, after Edgar's death, Morris Cleveland.

I never knew any of it, Dorcas thinks. *I'm almost fifty-six years old, and I feel as though I'm meeting my mother for the first time!*

She rereads the parts about Nicholas and the section on Morris.

It's almost noon when Dorcas lays aside the notebooks and rushes to her mother's apartment. Lavinia isn't at home. She heads next for the Trolley Stop, where she finds Lavinia in the midst of a tuna sandwich and a deep conversation with Wanda.

"Will you join me for lunch, Dorcas?" Lavinia asks, but Dorcas isn't interested in food.

"How about some iced tea, then?" Wanda suggests and pours her a glass before she moves on to another customer.

"Mother," Dorcas plunges in. "You don't need to do a thing to your memoirs. They're a treasure exactly the way they are, and I can't begin to thank you for letting me read them. I know Sasha will cherish them."

"Maybe she'll turn them into a film," Lavinia suggests with a wicked smile. "But all the actresses I'd want to play me in my younger days are either dead or over the hill. I was thinking Bacall or Hepburn. And who would play Nicholas, do you think?"

Dorcas laughs at her irrepressible mother but then grows serious again. "Mother, there's something I need to ask you about Nicholas." She fiddles with the wrapper on her straw. "What do you think would have happened if you had married him?"

Lavinia leans across the table, her blue eyes close to Dorcas's. "A disaster!" she declares. "A few glorious months and then unmitigated disaster! Why, I didn't even *know* him. And we were from different worlds, Dorcas. We had nothing in common, except being young and lusty."

Like Toby, Dorcas concedes. *What did I really know about him? That would have been a disaster too, in all probability.*

"But," Lavinia continues, "I got to paint my dreams, to make them come out the way I wanted. Better that way, sometimes."

Dorcas reaches across the table and takes her mother's two hands—blue-roped, brown-spotted, bony—and tenderly kisses them, first the left with its old-fashioned wedding band, then the right. "Absolutely," Dorcas agrees. For once, Lavinia doesn't pull away.

❧

That afternoon Dorcas finds a box for mailing Lavinia's notebooks and sits down at the kitchen table to write a note to go with them. *Dear Sasha,* she begins:

Lovey asked me to send you these notebooks, in which she's written what she calls her memoirs and what I'd call the story of the remarkable life of an unusual woman. I'm still marveling at what I learned. All I'll say now is that I had no idea what my mother was really like—so vibrant, so much more daring than I ever imagined! What she doesn't mention is that she probably won't be able to see well enough to paint for much longer—she's rapidly losing her sight. But you may know that.

There's something else I want to say to you—

But Dorcas isn't quite sure how to say it. She pours herself a glass of sun tea and carries the letter and the tea out to Caroline's Garden. Hummingbirds dart around the little statue, water splashes into the basin, the sweet smell of roses fills the air. Eventually her pen flies across the page.

There's something else I want to say to you, Sasha, and that is that you and Michelle are welcome to come here, if you decide to work out your relationship together. And I don't mean just as visitors. I'd like you to consider starting a life here—the three of you. You might find that Juniata is not such a bad place to live and to bring up your child.

I confess that this is not an unselfish invitation. I'd love to watch my grandson grow up while his parents share the newly created position of chef at Morgan House. You could stay in those two attic rooms until you find something that suits you better. Please, please think about it—it would make a grandmother and a great-grandmother very happy.

Dorcas reads over the letter, signs it—*My love to you both, Mom*—and puts it in the box with Lavinia's notebooks. She gets the package to the post office just before it closes.

That evening she considers calling Rod. Over supper— leftovers from the tarragon chicken Sasha had prepared— she has done some soul-searching and examined her anxieties. She knows she doesn't need another relationship—she likes being on her own, running a business, instead of continually yearning for somebody, some *man*. Running Morgan House has turned out to be strenuous, more than she anticipated, but does she want or need Rod to become involved any more than he already is? Lavinia will require more time and attention from her as her eyesight diminishes, and now Dorcas has invited Sasha and family to move into her life, too. Does she need another ingredient in this stew? Then there's Rootie—she would hate to damage that friendship.

On the other hand, she did promise Rod she'd invite him over for dinner. She has the medal to return to him. And they really should discuss plans for fixing up the stable. *Rod is no big deal,* she tells herself; *no big deal at all.*

For the first time, though, Dorcas wonders what her mother would do in her situation. The very notion makes her laugh out loud: *no question* what Lavinia would do!

She takes a deep breath and dials Rod's number. There's always the possibility that he won't be at home, or that he'll make some excuse to put her off.

But Rod answers on the first ring. She pictures him still damp from the shower after a long day at work, dressed in T-shirt and jeans, watching the evening news. He'd be happy to come, he says, and she detects a note of enthusiasm in his voice, almost a lilt. They settle on the following Wednesday.

Immediately practical, she decides to grill salmon steaks and find some fresh raspberries. Rod will bring the wine, and he's found a new recipe for olive bread that he wants her to try. She'll wear her blue linen shirt, nothing fussy.

And she won't mention it's her birthday.